✂ FIRST IMPRESSIONS ✂

Also by Marilyn Sachs
Lost in America

FIRST IMPRESSIONS

MARILYN SACHS

A Deborah Brodie Book
ROARING BROOK PRESS
New Milford, Connecticut

A Deborah Brodie Book
Published by Roaring Brook Press
Roaring Brook Press is a division of Holtzbrinck Publishing Holdings
Limited Partnership
143 West Street, New Milford, Connecticut 06776

Distributed in Canada by H. B. Fenn and Company, Ltd.

Library of Congress Cataloging-in-Publication Data

Sachs, Marilyn.
First impressions / Marilyn Sachs.— 1st ed.
  p. cm.
"A Deborah Brodie book."
Summary: Rereading Jane Austen's "Pride and Prejudice" over Christmas
break gives brainy fifteen-year-old Alice a different way of looking at
herself, her first boyfriend, her friends, and her family.
ISBN-13: 978-1-59643-117-1
ISBN-10: 1-59643-117-2
  [1. Interpersonal relations—Fiction. 2. Dating (Social customs)—Fiction.
3. Austen, Jane, 1775-1817. Pride and prejudice—Fiction. 4. Family life—
San Francisco (Calif.)—Fiction. 5. San Francisco (Calif.)—Fiction.] I.
Title.
  PZ7.S1187Fir 2006
  [Fic]—dc22
  2005020305

  10 9 8 7 6 5 4 3 2 1

Roaring Brook Press books are available for special promotions and
premiums. For details, contact: Director of Special Markets, Holtzbrinck
Publishers.

Book design by Patti Ratchford
Printed in the United States of America
First edition March 2006

For my daughter, Anne

FIRST IMPRESSIONS

CHAPTER 1

It was the C+ that brought about the magic.

"Calm down," said my teacher, Ms. Herran. "You aren't the first student to get a C+."

"But this is the first time for me. I've never gotten a grade below an A. Well, once in science back in middle school I got an A-."

Ms. Herran leaned forward. I noticed that she squinted even behind her glasses.

"I'm afraid you just didn't get it," she said gently. "*Pride and Prejudice* is one of the great comic novels. Jane Austen was a genius at irony, and you don't appear to realize that."

"Well, it seemed to me that *Pride and Prejudice* was really a tragedy that just got away from the author."

Ms. Herran shook her head, and squinted even more. "You're talking about a very great author, Alice. Most critics agree that part of her greatness was her control. It is certainly not a tragedy. And your paper . . . well I was kind in giving you a C+. If I didn't consider you an excellent student, you might have even gotten a D or worse."

"It's a tragedy," I insisted. "Sure, Elizabeth and Jane get their guys, and Lydia makes an exciting, scandalous marriage, and the author hopes that Kitty will turn out okay, but Mary . . . it's a tragedy for Mary."

"Oh, Alice, Mary is not really important. She's a minor character and a nerd. She provides comic relief."

"In the whole book, she's hardly mentioned. There are

five sisters, and at the end, only poor Mary is left, stuck with her mother, the scorn of her father, and the disinterest of everybody else."

I began choking up, and Ms. Herran looked away, embarrassed. I had been reading classics ever since fourth grade—*Oliver Twist, The Three Musketeers, the Odyssey, Jane Eyre, Ivanhoe*—and I never found myself upset about any character, not even Rebecca in *Ivanhoe*. "It's just not fair to leave Mary like that."

"I tell you what," Ms. Herran said. She patted my hand. "Don't take it so hard. Why don't you reread the book, and then write another paper? You'll have two weeks over Christmas, so if you would like to try again, and write a new paper, I'm sure you'll understand what I'm trying to explain. And I'll just change your grade."

"Okay," I told her. "I'll try."

CHAPTER 2

It is a truth universally acknowledged that the third child in a family of five is never appreciated.

"Alice, come and set the table!" yelled my mom.
"I'm studying. Why don't you ask Jeremy or Joey?"
'They're out playing soccer."
"Well, I'm reading a book for school."
"Come on down. We're having dinner early because Rosie is getting together with her jazz band to rehearse."
"So why can't she do it?"
"Alice!"

I'm not the favorite of anybody in my family. Maybe that's why I'm so upset about Mary. My mom is crazy about Rosie, my older sister, who is eighteen and plays the trombone in her high school band. My dad coaches my twin brothers, Jeremy and Joey, in soccer. They're just eleven. My father is a sports nut. If he's not working as a cop, he's coaching my brothers or watching sports on TV.

My other sister, Olivia, seventeen, is stunning. Even I'm willing to admit that. Her blonde hair shimmers when she walks, her green eyes turn from blue to green to yellow, depending on what she wears or what kind of mood she's in—cranky most of the time. So, her eyes are generally yellow–green. Her complexion is creamy, her mouth a pouty pink, and every other part of her fits together like a jigsaw puzzle. When she walks down the street, people turn and look at her.

My parents are so proud of Olivia they're willing to spend any amount of money to help her buy clothes and take lessons in modeling. She and I share a room, but she's too busy looking at herself in the mirror or going on diets to bother talking to me.

And then there's me. Let's get it over with right away. I'm not pretty. I mean, my eyes are in the right place, and so are all the rest of my features. But it all adds up to ordinary. I'm short, overweight, with plain brown hair and plain hazel eyes, and wide feet. Nobody turns to look at me when I walk down the street. But I'm smart—and wasted here in this family. Mom, who barely made it through high school, says I take after my father's family.

"They all think they're better than anybody else."

But Dad defends himself by pointing out that except for his brother, Harry, who's an accountant, nobody else graduated from college.

Once in a while, somebody offers help.

"Let me try a little makeup on you," Olivia suggested one day.

She sat me down in front of the mirror. Her lovely face above my own was a study in contrasts.

"First, I'll try pulling your hair back from your face . . . like this . . . No, I guess we'd better not show too much. Okay, maybe some eye shadow, and mascara . . . there." She worked on, murmuring encouraging words to herself. She slapped various smelly powders on my face and outlined my thin lips with lip liner to make them look fuller. "There!" she said finally.

There was me in the mirror, looking like me with makeup.

"Maybe a haircut," Olivia muttered, "or maybe if you grew out your bangs . . ."

My dad suggested sports. "Soccer would keep you in shape," he said. "There's a girls' team at the Y."

"I don't like soccer," I told him.

"Well, what about basketball? You're not very tall, but if you're fast—"

"I'm not fast."

Finally, he suggested tennis, but after spending a couple of Saturdays with me at the tennis courts in the park, he gave up.

Mom tries to look brave when I show her my report card, which generally has all A's. If somebody congratulates her on the fact that I got into Lowell, the academic school in San Francisco, she says almost apologetically, "She studies a lot."

Once, she sat down next to me when I was reading and asked, "What book is that?"

"Oh, it's *Crime and Punishment* by Dostoyevsky."

"Who?"

"Dostoyevsky. He was Russian."

"It's a very big book."

"I don't mind."

Mom shook her head. "You need to get out more," she said. "You always have your nose in a book. Don't you have any friends who like to have a good time?"

"But I am having a good time. And most of my friends at school are like me."

No way was I going to put up with a C+—it would affect my final grade. So, I had no choice but to accept Ms. Herran's offer and try to reread the stupid book with an open mind. But I kept looking for Mary. In the book, they go to a ball, and the two youngest sisters, Lydia and Kitty, dance every dance while Jane, the oldest and the most beautiful, dances with Mr. Bingley. And the two of them pretty much fall in love. Elizabeth is spurned by Mr. Darcy. And where is Mary? What is she feeling while, obviously, nobody is asking her to dance?

There, over there, in the shadows, Mary sits. Jane Austen has forgotten all about her, but I find her on page 8, just at the point where the book says, *"Mr. Bingley had soon made himself acquainted with all the principal people in the room; he was lively and unreserved, danced every dance . . ."* but not with Mary.

She's probably wearing a high-necked dress of a dull color, and she's trying to look indifferent. But she's suffering. I can feel her suffering from in between those sentences that leave her out.

I slammed the book shut.

"Alice," my mother shouted, "can you run out to the store and pick up some apple juice? I'm all out, and you know Joey won't drink anything else lately."

"So, tell *him* to go."

"He's not home."

"Well, why don't you ask Rosie?"

"Alice, I'm asking *you!*"

It was raining, and I walked to the store muttering to myself about how unfair life was for Mary and me. There was only one other customer in the store—a woman in a hooded raincoat.

"Yes?" said the man behind the counter, smiling his customer smile. "What can I do for you?"

"Uh, where is the apple juice?" I asked.

"In the back of the store, with all the other juices." I

noticed that he didn't seem to be paying any attention to the woman in the raincoat.

At first, I couldn't find the apple juice. There was orange, grapefruit, even mango, but the apple juice wasn't in sight. I wondered what Mary drank, and somebody said, "Tea."

"What?"

The woman in the raincoat was standing a short distance away.

"It's down at the bottom of the shelf," she said in a strange accent, and sure enough, there it was.

I picked up a bottle and brought it to the counter. The clerk put my apple juice into a bag, smiled, and wished me a good day.

The woman in the raincoat was still there but he didn't notice her.

And that's when the magic began.

CHAPTER 3

It is never possible to ignore Christmas. Buying the right tree, decorating it, putting up lights, baking cookies, and planning for the big day, I was somewhat distracted from reading. There was also the question of presents.

Buying presents for the various members of my family always presented a problem. Last year, I bought a book for each of them. It was not a very successful choice. Only Joey seemed to open his. It was a book about baseball, and I know he at least looked at it, because I found it opened to the section with the photographs. The other books pretty much remained under the tree during the holidays, until Mom finally scooped them up and put them on the shelf in the kitchen along with her cookbooks. Around Easter they ended up in the pantry, where she keeps the soaps, Brillo pads, and ant traps.

This year, I decided to go shopping on the third day of the vacation. Get it over with, and then I could return to *Pride and Prejudice* later in the day. As usual, it was raining.

"Mom," I asked. "Can you give me a ride to the mall?"

"Now?"

"I want to do my Christmas shopping."

"Oh, well, okay then. I'm making crusts for the pecan and lemon pies, but I guess I can drop you. Take the bus back."

"Do you have any idea what I should get for Dad?"

"I bought him a sweater. You could get him . . . let me see. . . how about socks?"

"Mom, that's not much of a present for Christmas. It's so hard to buy for men."

Mom put her raincoat on. "Take an umbrella," she said. "And don't spend too much."

"I only have forty-four dollars. I can't spend too much."

"Here!" Mom put two ten-dollar bills into my hand.

"But, Mom, you don't have to," I protested weakly. Every year, Mom subsidized me, as I knew she subsidized every other kid in the family.

The mall was crowded with huge numbers of shoppers. A large, brilliant Christmas tree stood in the center court, with gleaming red, white, green, and blue balls. Silver and gold Christmas garlands hung on all the walls. Santa Claus was seated on a throne and smiling or weeping children waited to take photos with him.

People scurried everywhere—children laughed, babies cried, and grown-ups carried piles of clothing and toys in their arms. I wandered around, stopping in a variety of stores, but ending up finally in dependable old Macy's. In the junior department, I fingered a slinky black, see-through dress over a satin slip. I even carried it over to a mirror and held it tightly in front of me. Quickly, I put it back on the rack and began to focus on my shopping.

What to get? I had sixty-four dollars, thanks to my mom, to spend on six people.

"Hi, Alice," somebody said behind me.

"Oh, hi, Kevin. What are you doing here?"

"Trying to figure out what to get for my parents and my sister." He made a face. "I've been wandering around for maybe an hour, and I can't make up my mind."

I'd known Kevin Tanner since kindergarten. He was one of those boys you could feel perfectly comfortable with. Others, I had to admit, often made me feel uneasy, especially lately. Made me feel as if I wished they noticed me or maybe not noticed me, or maybe both at the same time. But Kevin was like an old glove that just fit comfortably.

"Gloves!" I said. "Get them gloves. As a matter of fact, that's what I'm going to do too. Thanks for giving me the idea."

"What idea?" Kevin's face assumed its usual perplexed expression. He was one of those people who seemed to approach most of the world as if he were surprised or confused. Which was one of the reasons he made me feel so comfortable.

Both of us bought gloves—bright green ones for my brothers, pretty pink-and-white ones for all our sisters, dark red ones for our mothers, and navy blue ones for our fathers. It took about fifteen minutes for the two of us to make our selections.

While we waited in the line at the gift-wrap counter, Kevin asked, "Have you got any special plans for the holidays?"

I made a face. "I have to reread *Pride and Prejudice*."

"Why would you want to do that?" Kevin looked even more perplexed.

"Because Ms. Herran gave me a C+ on my paper. I've never gotten a C+ ever before in my life. What did you get?"

Kevin avoided looking at me. "I got an A-."

"You mean you liked it?"

"Well, to tell you the truth, I didn't really read it. My sister, Eleanor, helped me write the paper. She's an English major at Berkeley, and she loves Jane Austen."

"I don't. I hate the book, but I hate getting a C+ even more. Ms. Herran said if I reread the book and wrote another paper, she might change my grade."

"I could ask my sister," Kevin said. "She's been in a good mood lately because she has a new boyfriend. She purposely wrote the paper kind of simple for me so Ms. Herran wouldn't be suspicious. But for you—"

"What for me?"

"Well, I mean, you're so smart, she wouldn't have to write it simple."

Kevin turned away his head, but I could see that suddenly he was uncomfortable. Kevin Tanner, uncomfortable with me! That was the first magic. Because I suddenly realized that he's a boy. And not a bad-looking one. And that he admired me. *Me!* I was even making him uncomfortable. I could not think of a single other boy who had ever noticed me long enough to become uncomfortable.

The line grew a little shorter. A woman whose present had just been wrapped passed us carrying a box laden with silver and gold bows, with red berries scattered all over it. I couldn't see her face, but she was wearing the same hooded raincoat she had worn in the grocery store.

My mind blurred. Things ran together—Kevin, the mysterious lady in the raincoat, the shortening line, the sounds of people in the store, the tearing of the wrapping paper, and the need to reply properly to Kevin.

"Uh, what kind of wrapping paper are you going to pick? Do you think that striped red and green would be good for our fathers and my brothers?"

Kevin's puzzled face began to make me feel I had handled matters correctly.

"See? Up there. And then we could pick the bright green paper with the red holly for our sisters. And . . . how about the shiny red paper with white bows for our mothers?"

Kevin no longer had a puzzled look on his face. It was definitely admiring. "You sure make your mind up fast," he said.

It took another half hour to get our presents wrapped.

"I just hate going home," I said. "I hate being stuck with that book for the rest of the afternoon." I stuffed my wrapped presents into a large shopping bag and reached out for—

"My umbrella! I lost my umbrella. Maybe I left it in the glove department. Did you notice my umbrella? It was a blue one."

"No, I didn't," Kevin said. "But if you want to go and look for it, leave your stuff here with me. I'll just wait for you to get back."

I hurried down to the glove department. No umbrella. None of the saleswomen had seen a lost umbrella. Maybe I hadn't even taken it from home. Maybe I had left it in Mom's car.

"I couldn't find it," I told Kevin. He was sitting on a bench near the phones. "I don't have enough money to buy one. I'm not so worried about me getting wet, but I'd hate to ruin all the pretty wrappings."

"My sister is picking me up," Kevin mumbled. "I just called her. We could drop you off. She said it was okay."

I looked down at Kevin. "That's really very nice of her—I mean, of you too."

"It's nothing." Kevin waved his hand.

"I live on—"

"I know where you live," Kevin said, looking down at the stuff we'd bought. "It's 745 Cleveland. It's just a few blocks from my house."

I looked down at the packages too. He knew my address, and he thought I was smart. Kevin had even asked his sister to give me a ride, before I had asked for one. Now I was uncomfortable too.

"She should be here in fifteen minutes or so. We could go downstairs and wait inside the front of the store," Kevin said.

It took less than five minutes to get ourselves downstairs with all our presents. Now we had about ten minutes to stand there and wait.

"Thanks," Kevin said.

"What for?"

"For helping me pick out Christmas gifts for my family."

"Well, you helped me too."

Maybe nine minutes to go now. Both of us looked intently out the entrance into the rainy parking lot. I tried to think of something interesting to say.

"I really hate that book," I said finally. "I don't know why anybody thinks it's a classic."

"I could ask my sister if you like, or, or, I mean, I could . . . could read it myself, but I guess you wouldn't be interested in what I have to say."

"Oh, no," I said fervently. "I'd really be interested in what you had to say. But it's not fair to ask you to make such a sacrifice."

"No, no, I'd like to. And I was even thinking, that is, if you have the time, you could bounce some of your ideas off me. We have nearly two weeks before the Christmas vacation ends."

"Eleven days," I said grimly.

"Well, why don't we get together in a few days," Kevin said boldly. "Here, I'll write down my telephone number on this piece of paper"—he tore a piece off my shopping bag—"and you can call me when you're ready."

What with talking about where we should go to discuss the book, and my warning him how much he'd hate it, the time passed quickly. His sister and her boyfriend drove up, and we hurried out.

Kevin and I sat in the backseat while Eleanor and Elton talked and laughed in the front. Kevin and I were silent, but I felt so overwhelmed and so happy, I was grateful for the silence. Thanks to *Pride and Prejudice*, Kevin and I were going out on a date—my first. Perhaps I should have been the one to have given him my telephone number instead of the other way around, but little details hardly mattered. He had asked me.

CHAPTER 4

Luckily, we always spend Christmas Day at my grandparents' house, so nothing much was expected of me beforehand. Mom baked her pies, Dad watched football, and Jeremy and Joey fought at home or played with their friends outside.

On the fourth day of the vacation, Rosie practiced with her jazz band from school downstairs in the family room. They were hoping to start their own band after graduating from high school, and they called themselves The Mothers, which didn't make sense since none of them were mothers, or fathers, either. The music reached every corner of our house.

"Can't you go someplace else?" Dad roared. "I can't hear a thing on TV."

Strangely enough, Mom enjoyed it. "I can remember myself when I was a girl. I played the trumpet in the school band, and I always thought I might even go professional. But then, with five kids . . ." Sometimes, if one or two of the musicians failed to show up, Mom could be persuaded to get out her old trumpet and join in. She actually didn't sound bad.

Olivia had her makeup spread out all over our room, even on my bed. I took my book and retreated to Rosie's room. I figured as long as she and her friends were down in the family room, I could enjoy a little privacy. She was the only one of us kids who had a room to herself. Maybe because she was the oldest or maybe because Mom liked her best. She hardly ever used it, which often provided a refuge for me.

I settled myself on her bed and opened the book to where I had left off. And that's where the magic *really* started.

Page 26. Jane, the oldest and prettiest sister, has been invited to dine with Mr. Bingley's sisters, Carolyn and Mrs. Hurst, who say that the gentlemen (Mr. Bingley and Mr. Darcy) will be dining with the officers and will not be present. Jane's mother, Mrs. Bennet, scheming to encourage a match between her daughter and Mr. Bingley, insists that Jane ride to Netherfield, Mr. Bingley's home, on horseback, instead of using their carriage, because she knows it will rain. She expects the ladies to invite Jane to stay overnight because of the weather. That way, Jane will see Mr. Bingley again.

In the morning, the rain has stopped. Jane sends a note saying that she is sick. Elizabeth, the heroine of the book, and the closest to Jane, insists on walking there to see her sister, in spite of the long walk and the muddy ground.

"'How can you be so silly,' cried her mother, 'as to think of such a thing, in all this dirt! You will not be fit to be seen when you get there.'"

The rest of the family gets into the discussion, and *Mary* says, *"I admire the activity of your benevolence . . . but every impulse of feeling should be guided by reason; and, in my opinion, exertion should always be in proportion to what is required."*

As usual, nobody listens to her. The two younger girls go off to chase the officers in Meryton while Elizabeth walks the three miles to Netherfield.

I closed the book. I thought of Mary, the only one of the five sisters at home, maybe reading a book or practicing a piece on her piano. The sounds of my sister's band penetrated the room even with the door closed. I shut my eyes, and suddenly, I hear only the tinkle of Mary's piano keys. And I'm right there, sitting next to her.

She is wearing a dull mouse-colored jumper over a white blouse, and I can see her profile as she hums along with her music. She isn't very pretty, her nose is too broad, her eyes too small, and her complexion pale and spotty. Her hair is messy, and she bites her fingernails. I sit down next to her and listen to her play. She isn't very good, and even I, who know very little about music, can tell. But she smiles and continues to hammer away.

"Wanna take a walk?" I ask her.

But she doesn't hear me. She doesn't know I'm there. I continue to listen to her play, and try to think of ways I can stop her. I make a few helpful suggestions, but she doesn't hear me

I open my eyes. The roar of Rosie's band brought me back to today. What happened? Did I fall asleep? I must have, I thought, and I picked up the book again.

Mary is not mentioned again until page 63, when her four sisters and their silly cousin, Mr. Collins, decide to walk to Meryton. Mary stays home.

I read on. And then it happens again. On page 89. Mr. Bingley has given a ball and distinguishes Jane so much that Mrs. Bennet doesn't stop talking, very loudly, about her expectations that Jane will soon be married to Mr. Bingley. What a good thing it will be, she tells anybody who will listen, because it will throw her other daughters *in the way of other rich men.* Other than Elizabeth and Jane, the whole Bennet family, especially Mary, make themselves so ridiculous that it appears everybody else in the room despises them. I can't help gritting my teeth. Mary insists on playing and singing in a thin, off-key voice and doesn't seem to plan on stopping, until her own father interrupts, saying, *"That will do extremely well, child. You have delighted us long enough. Let the other young ladies have time to exhibit."*

Mary is humiliated, and I know I have to step in. I am not going to allow it. And what's more, I am not going to let her play.

There she is, in an ill-fitting wine-colored gown that doesn't do anything for her mousy complexion, gathering up her music on her way to the piano, when I pass by and spill my glass of punch right on her dress.

"Oh, I'm so sorry," I say, and try to mop away at her with my napkin.

Mary looks around, wondering how it happened, since she wasn't drinking punch, but then others, including Mrs. Bennet and Mr. Bingley's sisters, are hovering around her, mopping away at her dress. One of Mr. Bingley's sisters, Mrs. Hurst, is about Mary's height, and after several significant looks by her brother, she offers to lend Mary a dress. Mary accompanies her upstairs.

Meanwhile, I sit off to the side and listen as all the other young ladies perform. Some of them are even worse than Mary, but a few are better, like Carolyn Bingley.

By the time Mary and Mrs. Hurst return, nobody else is playing, and the dancing has resumed. Mary is wearing one of Mrs. Hurst's dresses, a pretty pink one with white lace at the low bodice. She is flushed by all the sudden attention and doesn't look quite so plain. Mrs. Hurst quickly rejoins her own party, and for a few moments, Mary stands alone by the doorway. I am trying to think of what I could do to help her, but suddenly one of the officers stands in front of her. She seems startled, and then nods, yes. Together, the two of them join the line of dancers, and for the first time in the book, Mary dances.

While Mary is dancing, I examine each of the other characters. Of course, nobody is aware of my presence. Jane is dancing with Mr. Bingley. She is certainly pretty, with her soft light brown hair and large blue eyes, but not as pretty as my sister Olivia. She does, however, have a sweet and gentle manner. Elizabeth is talking to her friend Charlotte Lucas. Elizabeth is slim, with dark, curly hair and bright dark eyes. She is the heroine of the book and will marry the rich, handsome Mr. Darcy by the end of the story. At present, he is glaring at her. I am angry with her because she never helps Mary.

"Hi, Alice," somebody says.

I turn, and there is Kevin, dressed in a scarlet coat and all the rest of the uniform of a British soldier, circa 1811.

"What are you doing here?" I ask.

"Well, this is the part I'm up to in the book."

"You're too young to be a soldier."

"And you're too young to be wearing a dress like *that*," he says, grinning.

I look down and see a lot of skin. A form-fitting pale blue Empire dress clings more closely to my body than the dress I checked out at Macy's ever could.

"It's not my fault," I tell him. "I only came here to help Mary. Nobody can see me anyway."

"I can see you," Kevin said. "But, hey, why don't we join the dance? It looks like fun."

"I don't know what kind of dance it is," I say. "Actually, I've never danced in my life."

"Neither have I," Kevin says. "But none of this is real, so I imagine we'll be able to dance."

He holds out a hand to me, and I take it.

"Let's squeeze our way next to Mary," I suggest, "and see how she's doing."

By now, Mary is dancing with an officer named Denny, one of Lydia's admirers. She seems to be light and graceful on her feet. Denny is doing most of the talking, while she concentrates on the dance. I would like to ask her if she is enjoying herself, but aside from the fact that she wouldn't hear me, I am afraid she might say, as she does elsewhere in the story, *"I should infinitely prefer a book."*

❧ CHAPTER 5 ❧

I called Kevin the same day. When he picked up the phone, there was some loud yelling in the background. It sounded very much like my own house.

"What's going on?" I asked.

"Oh, wait! Let me go into the bathroom. It's always quieter in there."

I could hear a door closing, and Kevin said, "Hello."

"Hello. I'm still here. What's happening?"

"Nothing special. My sister had laundry going and went off with her boyfriend. The machine overflowed, and my mom is mad because now there's water all over the floor, and she wants Eleanor to clean it up."

"Sounds familiar," I said. "Anyway, I wondered if you—"

"No, Alice, I've only gotten up to the Netherfield Ball. Actually, I like the book—so far. But it's going to take me a few more days to finish it. I'm sorry."

"Kevin, I just wondered. Did something happen—I mean, something unusual—when you read that chapter?"

"Funny you should ask, because my father brought home a new DVD player, and he wanted me to help him install it. Just as I finished that chapter. That's why I had to stop reading."

He wasn't part of the magic. The magic in the book. No scarlet jacket. No dancing. It was happening only to me, in my own head.

"Alice? You still there? Look, it stopped raining. If you want to go for a walk somewhere, we can talk a little about the book—I mean, the part I've read so far. If you're not busy. Or maybe you want to wait until I'm finished."

"That's okay. It really is a nice day. I should get out, and I'll be very interested to hear what you have to say."

"Great. Let's walk on the beach. I'll come by, what, is half an hour okay?"

"Sure, I'll be ready."

Quickly, I changed into a different pair of jeans, pulled on another black shirt, and changed my socks. "Are you going somewhere?" my sister Olivia asked. She and her friends were off to the mall to buy new dresses for a New Year's Eve party one of them was giving.

"I'm going out," I said, pretending to be casual.

"Out? Who with?"

"A boy named Kevin Tanner. We're going to take a walk on the beach."

Olivia looked me up and down. "Those jeans are too baggy," she said. "Put on your black ones."

"They're tight."

"Wear them anyway."

"I can hardly move in them."

"What difference does that make? Change your jeans."

But the doorbell rang. Talk about embarrassing families. Olivia came downstairs with me. Jeremy and Joey had each other in a headlock on the floor, and Mom was shouting as she opened the door, "Alice, can you run over to the post office and get some stamps—oh!"

Kevin stood outside the door, blinking.

"Hi, Kevin," I said. "Let me just get my jacket."

"Is your sister Eleanor Tanner?" Olivia asked over my shoulder.

Kevin nodded.

"I know her. As a matter of fact, her boyfriend's cousin is my new boyfriend."

"What new boyfriend?" Mom demanded. "I never heard about a new boyfriend."

"This is my mother, my sister Olivia, and down there on the floor are my brothers, Jeremy and Joey. And this is my friend Kevin Tanner. Well, bye, everybody, I'll see you later."

As I closed the door behind me, Mom and Olivia were arguing about Olivia's new boyfriend.

"I guess I'm lucky," Kevin said.

"Lucky?"

"Yes. I only have one sister, and you have two and two brothers."

"How did you know that?"

Kevin shrugged and looked off into space. "I guess I know a lot about you, Alice."

And that was magic too.

We took off our sneakers and socks and walked barefoot on the warm, wet sand. I decided to tell him.

"Something happened to me today while I was reading *Pride and Prejudice*. You're going to think I'm crazy, but in that chapter, the Netherfield ball, it was suddenly as if I were in the book, and . . . and you were too."

"That happens to me sometimes too," Kevin said. "I like science fiction, and sometimes, especially when I'm reading Robert Heinlein, I almost feel I'm in outer space."

"But you were there too," I said. "And I changed things. I stopped Mary from playing. I poured punch on her dress so she had to go and change. And then one of the officers asked her to dance."

Kevin laughed. "The whole book would have been different if that had happened."

"What do you mean?"

But Kevin had picked up something on the beach, a sand dollar, a shell of some marine animal or other, and began talking about it.

He picked up a number of different shells that day as we walked along, and told me he wanted to be a marine biologist. He said he worried about the depletion of fish in the oceans due to pollution and overfishing.

"And what about you?" he asked. "What are you interested in?"

"I don't know yet."

"That's because you're good at so many things."

The sun was warm on our heads, the sea sparkled, and Kevin kept picking up shells or pieces of shells and explaining what kind of marine animal they belonged to. I'm not sure I heard everything he said, but it felt so good, so comfortable, I forgot all about *Pride and Prejudice.* Our shoulders frequently brushed, and I was aware that his head was a few inches above my own.

"Hi, Alice! Hi, Kevin!" two girls called out—Jamie Hsu and Robin Heller, classmates of ours, walking an ugly little gray dog. Jamie's face had a look of amazement that made me feel smug. She was obviously wondering why Kevin, why *any* boy, would be interested in walking with me on the beach.

"Hi, Jamie, Robin!" I shouted as loud as I could.

Kevin kept talking about mollusks. We must have walked miles before each of us realized it was beginning to grow dark.

"We'd better turn back," I told him.

"Okay," he said, "but I'm sorry. I guess I haven't been much help to you."

"What do you mean?"

"I mean we were supposed to talk about *Pride and Prejudice,* and here I've been just going on and on about myself."

"That's fine," I told him. "I'm glad to get away from the book, to tell you the truth."

"Well, I'll try to finish it, I promise. Tonight I'll just sit down and read."

"It's okay," I told him. "You've really helped me."

"How?" he wanted to know.

I didn't tell him, but when he said the whole book would have been different, after I told him how I had stopped Mary from playing the piano, I knew what I had to do. Kevin would not be part of it, but maybe he could—would—be part of my real world.

Off in the distance, I saw her as we walked back. She was facing the waves, so I couldn't see her face. But she was wearing the same long, hooded raincoat. I didn't mention it to Kevin, who was asking me if I would like to go with him to the aquarium. There was a particularly interesting exhibit of fish that swim so deep down in the water that no light penetrates the darkness, and they are blind.

I knew I would see the mysterious woman again, and I knew who she was.

Kevin called me that night while I was reading *Pride and Prejudice*. He wanted to figure out a date to see the exhibit at the aquarium. We ended up talking so long that Olivia stomped fiercely back and forth past me, pointing to her watch and then to herself.

When I ignored her and kept on talking to Kevin, she stalked off to the living room and began arguing with my mother.

"I keep telling you!" Olivia shouted, "I need a new cell phone. It's not fair for Alice to monopolize this phone!"

"You lost the last two cell phones," my mother said. "I told you if you want another one, you'll have to pay for it."

"I did not lose it!" Olivia shrieked. "It was Joey or maybe Jeremy who stole it out of my backpack. And Rosie never lets me use hers."

"Stop shouting at me!" shouted my mother.

My father began complaining that he couldn't watch his program and that Olivia should calm down.

"Is somebody upset in your family?" Kevin asked.

"Somebody is always upset in my family," I told him.

Kevin laughed. "You're funny," he said. "I mean, I always knew you were smart, but I never thought you were funny."

"Neither did I," I told him. "But Thursday is fine. I should be finished with the book by then, so I'll have plenty of time. I probably won't write a very long report."

"I'll try to finish it too, Alice. Maybe I'll call you if I do. Would that be okay?"

"Oh, yes," I said. "And maybe I can manage to read a little

bit about fish before we see the exhibit."

"Alice!" my mother called. "Please get off the phone."

"Well, I guess I should go."

"Yeah," Kevin said. "Well, bye."

"Bye."

"Oh, and what's a good time on Thursday?"

"Anytime is okay. What's a good time for you?"

"How about two?"

"That's fine, or we could go earlier."

"Alice, will you get off the phone! You've been talking for thirty-seven minutes," Olivia shouted.

"Well, I guess you have to go. Let's say two, then."

"I guess I do. And I'll be ready at two. Should we meet at the aquarium?"

"No, I'll stop by for you. We can go together."

"Alice!"

I hurried off to Rosie's room and closed the door. I leaned against it and thought about Kevin. I didn't want to do anything else but think about Kevin. Was he thinking about me? Was he looking forward to Thursday at two the way I was?

So many boys I had thought about, daydreamed about—boys who hardly knew I was alive. But Kevin knew I was alive. Kevin—

"Alice, are you in there?" my mother said outside the door.

"Oh! Yes, Mom." I opened the door. My mother stood there, smiling at me. "So, you're going out with Kevin Tanner?" she asked.

"Well, sort of," I said vaguely. "I mean, he's trying to help me with my book report, and . . ."

"And?"

"We're going to see an exhibit on blind fish at the aquarium."

"Blind fish?"

"Well, he wants to be a marine biologist, and he's very interested in fish."

"Now, Alice," said my mother, entering the room and motioning for me to sit down next to her on Rosie's bed. "I think we need to have a little talk."

"About what?"

My mother patted my arm. "You've never gone out with a boy before, and I know Kevin is a very nice boy—comes from a decent family—but he is a boy, and—"

"Mom," I said, "are you going to talk to me about the birds and the bees? Give me a break! We learn all that stuff in school nowadays."

"Well, Alice, I just want you to know that you're much too young to even be thinking of such a thing."

"What thing? Mom, Kevin and I are friends. We're going to an exhibit on blind fish. I'm not thinking about anything but that. And now I have to go back to reading *Pride and Prejudice* because I need to get that paper written before the end of the vacation."

"Yes, that's right," said my mother, jumping up, plainly relieved. "Go read your book. That's a good idea. Work on your report. Keep busy. That's always a good idea."

I ended up back in my room. Olivia was still on the phone. I checked my watch. She must have been talking more than forty-five minutes. *Pride and Prejudice* was lying upside down on my bed. I picked it up and settled myself on the bed. Did Mrs. Bennet ever talk to her daughters about birth control? She certainly didn't have to worry about Mary.

Page 104. Elizabeth has joined Lydia and Kitty on a walk to Meryton. But where is Mary? I don't hear her tinkly sounds on the piano. I look around the house for her. Mrs. Bennet is busy complaining to Hill, the housekeeper; Jane is writing a letter; Mr. Bennet is reading in his library. So where is Mary?

She's not in the house. I hurry after the other girls, and, surprise, Mary is with them, walking to Meryton. She is speaking to Elizabeth, who is nodding and plainly not listening. Mary looks almost pretty. She is wearing a white dress with yellow and violet flowers, and a new bonnet, trimmed with a violet-colored ribbon. I hurry up and join them.

As soon as they reach Meryton, Lydia and Kitty become boisterous, showing off because they see the officers in the distance. Elizabeth tells them to behave, although she is looking around herself. A bunch of officers are standing across the road, speaking to that lady in the hooded raincoat.

Lydia shouts and waves.

"Stop it," Elizabeth whispers. But she is smiling because she sees Mr. Wickham, who is the villain of the story. At the moment, Elizabeth has a crush on him, and he appears to feel the same way about her. The officers approach and bow to the young ladies. They curtsey. I do too, but nobody notices. Mr. Wickham offers his arm to Elizabeth, and a couple of other officers walk off with Lydia and Kitty.

Poor Mary stands there alone for a moment, before Denny hurries over and offers her his arm. She smiles, and the two of them stroll off after the others. Which leaves only me alone now, wondering if I should follow them.

"Hi, Alice," says a voice. It's Kevin, dressed again in a scarlet uniform.

"You're not supposed to be here," I tell him.

"Why not?"

"Well, you're just a figment of my imagination. You pretty much told me that yourself."

"But, whatever, I'm here anyway." He offers me his arm, and I take it.

"We don't have to go off with the others," he says. "We could take a walk in the country. The woods around here are lovely."

"But I'm supposed to be taking care of Mary."

"It looks as if she's doing just fine all by herself."

Kevin's arm moves down my own, and suddenly we're holding hands as we walk out of Meryton.

"Are you sure Mary will be okay?" I ask feebly. "I'm supposed to watch her, and make sure she doesn't mess up."

"Why don't you watch *me*?" Kevin says, squeezing my hand.

Now the book, with my help, was really getting exciting. I forgot about Mary. Even when Mom called up to say dinner was ready, I stalled for as long as I could. I certainly didn't want to stop reading.

CHAPTER 7

Rosie, Olivia, and I shared a Mac. I used it almost exclusively for research. Olivia used it mostly for instant messaging or sending e-mails to her friends. Rosie was always yelling that she needed her own computer, but she hardly ever used it when it was available. The boys had their own computer to play computer games on.

After Mom had her little birds-and-bees discussion with me, it occurred to me to look up birth-control methods in Jane Austen's time—the early nineteenth century. I waited for an afternoon when Olivia was out with her friends, and Rosie was blasting away downstairs with some of the kids in her band. The band had been invited to perform on Valentine's Day at Great America, so our house was noisier than ever.

Birth control! One day, I would be using it. Obviously, Mom and Dad hadn't been very successful at it if Rosie and Olivia were only a year apart, and I was a year and a half younger than Olivia. Maybe after me, they learned something, because the boys were four and a half years younger than I was.

I Googled "Birth Control, nineteenth century." Vast numbers of entries appeared. It was difficult to decide where to begin.

An ancient Roman physician wrote the first book on contraception. He favored birth-control recipes made from fruits and nuts. But the big development came in the nineteenth century, with the use of a condom made from sheep intestines.

"What *are* you looking at, Alice?" Olivia asked, peering over my shoulder.

"Oh—Olivia—I didn't hear you come in."

Olivia laughed. "I can see why, but Alice, I had no idea Kevin was in such a hurry."

"Listen, Olivia," I said frantically, "it has nothing to do with Kevin. I'm doing a book report, and I needed some research."

Olivia patted my head. "Oh, sure!"

"Well, I just wondered . . . you know I'm reading *Pride and Prejudice*, which was written in the early nineteenth century, and I was just curious. . . ."

Olivia closed the door and sat down next to me. "Alice," she said, "you're too young, but—"

"Olivia, I swear I'm not . . . I mean, it's not for me." My face must have been turning all shades of red.

She wasn't listening. "Alice, wait until you're older. Maybe a year or two, and maybe with somebody older, a little more experienced than Kevin Tanner."

"Olivia, you've got it all wrong. Mom started talking to me. She doesn't think I know anything, so it gave me the idea of looking up—"

Olivia waved her hand. "It's okay, Alice. I'm glad you're interested. I guess you're just a late bloomer. But honey, don't rush into sex."

"Olivia! Kevin and I are going to see an exhibit on blind fish tomorrow. Honestly, this has nothing to do with him."

Olivia laughed out loud. "Fish eyes! That's the most original one I've ever heard. But anyway, take it easy, Alice, and talk to me first."

I escaped to the basement and sat down in front of the washing machine and dryer. As usual, both were running. But nobody else was there, and I could think.

Did Kevin ever think of me as more than a friend? Was it possible that one day, I would be interested in having sex? I wanted to talk to somebody—but who? In school, the sex education course explained all about how the sperm meets the egg and how the baby grows inside the mother's uterus. But nothing about the tingling, and how complicated and embarrassing the whole subject was.

"Alice," Mom shouted. "Where are you?"

"Oh, down in the basement, Mom."

"What's wrong with the washing machine?"

"Uh, I don't know."

Mom came running down the stairs. "Can't you hear that knocking?" She opened the door of the washing machine. "Just look," she said. "Joey put one of his sneakers in the laundry basket, and I must have dropped it in the washer. That boy loses everything," she said. "Anyway, Alice, while you're here, why don't you unload the dryer?"

"Okay," I said pleasantly, happy she didn't ask me what I was doing in the basement.

"They're mostly your clothes and Olivia's, with maybe a couple of Rosie's shirts, so you may as well take them upstairs, fold them, and put them away."

"Oh, sure, Mom," I said, filling up the basket and hurrying upstairs to our room.

Olivia was laughing out loud as I returned to our room, and the computer was making its usual IMing sounds.

I began folding the clothes, and gradually felt more comfortable. One of my pairs of jeans had a big tear over the right knee, so anything I had learned about birth control would have to wait until I figured out what to do about that. For the time being, at least, I didn't have to worry. And neither did Mary. Or Kevin.

CHAPTER 8

Jenny called me that night, and said, "Hi, Alice, what's up?" in a voice that sounded reproachful.

"Oh, Jenny, I've been meaning to call you. But—"

"I know. You've been busy. I bumped into Robin Heller yesterday, and she told me she saw you walking on the beach the other day with Kevin Tanner."

Jenny Chu was my best friend—sort of. She and I had lunch together at school, sometimes alone and sometimes with her dorky cousin, Cindy. Sometimes Jenny and I studied together in the library, and once in a while, we went shopping together at Stonestown or even to a movie.

She was very smart. Both of us had 4+ averages, but we were seldom in the same classes, which was good. Competition doesn't help a friendship.

"Yes, I meant to tell you but—"

"I didn't even know you were interested in him. You never said anything."

"It just happened. I was shopping in Macy's for Christmas presents, and he was there, and we started talking, and it was raining, so . . ." I rambled on and on, feeling guilty. I didn't know why I felt guilty, but I did.

"I told you how I felt about Sean Murray, and you said you didn't have time to think about boys. You said—"

"Well, it just happened, and I was going to call you, but, Jenny, I don't know why you're making such a big deal about it."

"I'm not making a big deal. I'm just wondering why Robin Heller, who isn't even a friend of yours, should be the one who tells me. Cindy says friends have to be open with each other. Cindy says—"

"I don't care what Cindy says. I don't even like Cindy!" I yelled.

"You don't like Cindy?" Jenny said. "How come all of a sudden you don't like Cindy?"

"Well, she's your cousin, but you're the one who's always complaining about her. You said your mother insisted you hang out with her, and you said she's pushy and keeps flirting with Sean. Anyway, let's stop arguing over nothing."

A pause.

"What are you doing now?" Jenny finally asked.

"Oh, I'm rereading *Pride and Prejudice*. Herran gave me a C+, but she said if I wrote a new paper, she might change my grade."

"I'm glad I don't have her," Jenny said, sounding more like herself.

"What about you? What are you doing?"

"Nothing much. I have to work on my report for Euro, and finish reading *Catcher in the Rye*."

Another pause.

Then I said, "Listen, Jenny, Kevin and I took a walk on the beach, and we're going to the aquarium tomorrow to see an exhibit on blind fish. And that's all."

"Well, Cindy and I are going to the movies tomorrow. I was going to ask you to come along, but—"

"I could the next day."

"Cindy is busy the next day, and I'm planning to go shopping with my mom for Christmas presents. Anyway, Alice, I was wondering if Kevin knows Sean Murray."

"I don't know if he does. I could ask him if you want me to."

"I just thought . . . if he knew him . . . maybe the four of us . . ."

"Jenny, I don't think I'm at that stage with Kevin. We're not really dating. We're just going to an exhibit of blind fish. But . . . well, if things move along, I will ask him."

"Thanks, Alice, and I'm sorry if I sounded cranky. I didn't mean to."

"It's okay, Jenny. I shouldn't have lost my temper either."

After I hung up, I sat there thinking about Jenny. Was she really my best friend? In fifth grade, I had a friend who I could honestly say was my best friend—Rachel London. She and I played together almost every day after school. Of course, she lived just a few blocks away. We studied together, read the same books, had sleepovers, and stuck up for each other if some other kid picked on one of us. But she and her family moved away to Kansas City. We promised that we would always be best friends. In the beginning, we e-mailed and called. But in less than a year, we weren't in touch at all. I'd almost forgotten what she looked like.

But I knew that had been a real friendship, and that Jenny and I were really just school friends. We had lunch together, talked about our teachers, and mostly put up with Cindy. Sometimes, when we were alone, I almost felt that our friendship could blossom into something better.

She confided in me about Sean Murray. If we were closer, I would have told her what I really thought—that he was so cute almost any girl in the school would have a crush on him. He always seemed to be walking along the halls with some girl trailing along. It would have been hard, but if we really were best friends, I would have told her.

Jenny was short, slim, and had shiny black hair. Otherwise, like me, she wasn't anything special to look at. Sure, she was smart, but I wasn't sure that Sean Murray would be interested in a smart girl.

I never saw Kevin with a bunch of girls surrounding him. He certainly was a whole lot different from Sean.

I tried to stay focused on my friendship with Jenny, but my mind kept drifting off to Kevin.

CHAPTER 9

Christmas! Even though I tried hard to wake up earlier than anybody else in my family so that I could continue reading *Pride and Prejudice*, it proved impossible. Jeremy and Joey's loud shrieks and scampering up and down the stairs woke all of us.

The tradition in my family is for everybody to gather around the tree before the presents are opened. Only one present can be opened at a time, and the rest of us are expected to exclaim, "Oh, what a great present," or "Isn't that perfect!"

I had to admit that my interest in reading was temporarily suspended. Everybody in my family looked so lovable in their robes, pajamas, and uncombed hair, I was almost happy to be part of them. Only Olivia had managed to brush her wonderful hair and apply lipstick. She was wearing a white silk robe with red flowers that my parents had given her last Christmas.

Joey and Jeremy always received exactly the same gifts, in the same colors, from my parents. One year, Joey had been given a blue sweater and Jeremy a green. The resulting havoc had convinced my parents to avoid the advice of experts to treat identical twins as separate individuals. This year, they gave the boys each an identical white basketball, and a hoop to hang up on the lamp pole in front of the house. Rosie gave them computer games that they could play together.

My gifts of gloves were received with polite if not enthusiastic approval. Olivia's gifts of comb-and-brush sets were accepted with a similar lack of fervor. Rosie gave us CDs of her group, and the boys actually, and most originally, managed to find unusual candles for each of us—a lion candle for Dad, a bright red rose for Mom, a panther for Rosie, a bunch of purple grapes for Olivia, a cute little white cat for me.

"They're beautiful!" I exclaimed, really pleased.

"Where did you get them?" asked Mom. "I know you didn't want to go shopping with me." She narrowed her eyes just slightly. "They look like expensive candles. You didn't even want any money from me. Where did you get them?"

"We worked for them," Jeremy said proudly. "We walked Mrs. Lucas's dogs, we fed her rabbit, and we cleaned the hutch."

"Who?" demanded my mother.

"Mrs. Lucas. She's our friend Ben's neighbor, and she makes candles. She's a very nice lady, even though Ben doesn't like her. She says we can keep working for her, and she'll pay us with money."

"Hmm!" Mom said. "I'd like to meet her."

But the rest of us were too busy unwrapping presents to worry about Mrs. Lucas's motives. My parents gave Rosie a charm bracelet. They gave Olivia another cell phone, and me a pale blue sweater.

Olivia kissed Mom and Dad, warned Joey and Jeremy that they had better keep their hands off her phone, and disappeared to check what her other friends had received.

I found myself experiencing a total reversal of emotions on looking at the sweater. Before meeting Kevin, I would have considered it another article of clothing my mother gave me to make me appear more attractive. But now, I was seeing myself wearing the sweater when we went to the fish exhibit the next day.

"If you don't like it," my mother said, "you can exchange

it for another color. They had lovely shades of red, rose, and pink. I just thought this color would look good with your hazel eyes."

"No, it's just great, Mom," I said. "I really like it."

"You do?" Mom was clearly surprised. She had seldom given me anything I'd liked. "And I could lend you a short strand of pearls to wear with it. As a matter of fact, I could give them to you because I have another one. I'm sure Olivia or Rosie would never wear pearls."

"Yes," I said. "I would like pearls. Or maybe I should wear my gold locket Grandma gave me. I never do."

"Well, you should wear it today," said my mother. "She'd be pleased to see you wear it."

It was pleasant sitting there next to my mother, under the tree, with wrapping paper and ribbons all around us. Just the two of us, talking about jewelry. All the others had disappeared with their presents. Mom reached out and smoothed my hair back from my face.

"Do you need me to do anything, Mom?" I offered.

"No, darling." She smiled. "Dad's going to make his famous hash browns and eggs, and maybe the boys can help him for a change."

What a day! More presents from Grandma and Grandpa. Money. For the second year in a row, they had given us money. I could buy books, if I liked, maybe even one on fish. And the food was so delicious—stuffed turkey, ham, sweet potatoes, salad, Mom's pies, a box of See's chocolates brought by an aunt for my grandparents but shared with the rest of us. There were flowers from an uncle, cards from the younger cousins, tickets to an ice-skating show from Aunt Katie, and lots of noise and laughter. Joey and Jeremy played one of their computer games with our cousins Sally and Frank, both about their age.

Grandma smiled when she noticed that I was wearing the locket she'd given me. I wore an old red sweater, saving the blue sweater for the next day.

"Do you have anybody's pictures inside?" Grandma wanted to know.

"I haven't decided yet," I told her. "Too many kids in my family. I guess I could put in pictures of Mom and Dad."

Grandma nodded approvingly but didn't have a chance to respond because somebody in the kitchen was complaining that the gravy was boiling over.

After dinner, I retreated into Grandma and Grandpa's bedroom and settled myself on a chair at the side of the bed.

Page 193. Elizabeth has returned from a visit to her friend Charlotte Lucas (now Mrs. Collins). In the course of that visit, Mr. Darcy proposes to her, in a nasty way—pointing out how rich and important he is and how poor and undistinguished she is. She turns him down. Good for her! I'm beginning to approve of Elizabeth more and more. But I must not forget my responsibility to Mary.

On her way home, Elizabeth meets up with her sisters Jane, Kitty, and Lydia for the last lap of the journey. Lydia and Kitty make pests of themselves in the coach, and when they get home, on page 197, Lydia says to Mary, "*I wish you had gone with us, for we had such fun!*" . . . *Mary very gravely replied, 'Far be it from me, my dear sister, to depreciate such pleasures. They would doubtless be congenial with the generality of female minds. But I confess they would have no charms for me. I should infinitely prefer a book.'*

"But of this answer Lydia heard not a word. She seldom listened to any body for more than half a minute, and never attended to Mary at all."

I shook my head. It's hard to blame Lydia. Mary does make the most pompous, exasperating remarks. Perhaps my teacher, Ms. Herran, isn't entirely wrong.

I kept shaking my head over Mary's comments, and suddenly they disappeared from the page.

Yes, that's what I would have to do. Just like I stopped her from playing at the Netherfield Ball, I have to stop her from talking.

So, Mary doesn't say anything. As a matter of fact, Mary isn't even in the room, although nobody but me notices.

Where is she? I look in the other rooms. She's not there and not at the piano.

I go outside. It's a cloudy, cool day. I can't see Mary anywhere, but after a while, I hear voices. They're coming from the hedgerow that divides Mr. Bennet's property from the neighboring estate. I hurry over, and I find Mary walking with Denny.

She looks almost fetching in her white bonnet, pink dress, and short strand of pearls.

Denny is uncomfortable. "I find it very difficult," he says, "to think that my regiment will be leaving Meryton in a few days, and will be encamped at Brighton."

Mary sighs and says nothing. I nod approvingly. She's doing fine. As long as she keeps her mouth shut.

"You see," he continues, "I have grown very attached to Meryton, and . . . to . . . Perhaps you know what I mean?"

Mary shivers and looks up at him with just the perfect look of sorrow, helplessness, and admiration. I have certainly done a lot for her, I think proudly.

MARILYN SACHS

"You're cold," Denny says, taking off his cape and wrapping it around her shoulders. "Miss Bennet . . . Mary . . . may I call you Mary?"

She nods shyly. Good girl! Just don't say anything stupid.

"I know I can't expect you to write to me, but—"

"Alice?" somebody says. "I've been looking for you . . ."

Denny and Mary disappear behind a bend in the hedgerow.

"Kevin?" I say.

". . . all over the house," my father says. "What are you doing in here?" He eyes the book in my hand. "Oh, honey," he says reproachfully. "We're about to make our Christmas toast to Grandma and Grandpa. Everybody else is in the dining room. Can't you put that book down just for a few minutes? 'Atta girl!"

CHAPTER 10

I looked in the mirror the next morning and studied my eyes. Mom had said when she gave me the sweater that it would go with my eyes. I opened my eyes very wide and smiled, as if that would affect the color. They were sort of hazel, sort of brown, sort of nothing special. Olivia had blue eyes when she was happy—bright, sparkling ones—and my father had blue eyes, more or less. Middle-aged eyes have too many wrinkles and pouches around them for the color to really matter.

But when I put on the blue sweater, and looked at myself in the mirror, my eyes did appear to shine. Was I pretty? Well, maybe. I brushed my hair hard, in the front, on top, and in the back. If you looked very hard, there appeared to be a slight curl on the bottom.

I put on my tight black jeans and tried to sit down. If I sucked in my breath very hard, I could manage. And if I stood up straight, I could hobble around, but there was always the fear they would rip.

Love was one thing. Jeans were another. I pulled them off and put on my regular jeans. Even they felt snug. Too much eating at Christmas. But in the new year, I hoped food would not taste so good or that I would not always be so hungry.

It was eleven-thirty, and there I was, fully dressed. Kevin would not arrive until two. Wasn't it silly to spend the whole morning dressing myself just to wait for over two hours? What was the matter with me? Just because a boy paid a little attention to me, did I have to turn into a different person?

Mom's pearls lay on the dresser, next to my gold locket.

Grandma had asked me whose pictures were inside the locket, and I had mumbled something about Mom and Dad. But I knew whose picture I really wanted. I held up the locket in front of my blue sweater, and then I held up the pearls.

"Dorky!" said Olivia, standing behind me. "Nobody wears pearls or lockets. And put on your black jeans."

"They don't fit me," I told her. "If you like them, you can have them."

"I don't want them," she said. "The waist is too high up. Anyway, don't wear the pearls or the locket. Where are you going with Kevin?"

"I told you, to the aquarium. He wants to see an exhibit on . . . well, he's going to be a marine biologist, and he's interested in fish."

"I guess we should settle for just a little lipstick—sort of pale, and I could put some mousse in your hair. It would give it a little more shine. Have you kissed him yet?"

"Olivia, we're just friends."

"Some boys," Olivia reflected, as she rubbed gook into my hair, "don't know how to kiss. And some boys get spit all over you. I never go out with boys who get spit on me. There, doesn't that look nice?"

"Yes," I said, "it does look nice, but it smells funny."

"The smell will go away when it dries. Now, look at these old lipsticks of mine. Which color do you like? I guess this is a good one." Olivia picked up a pale pink. "I wouldn't be caught dead in that color, but it goes with that sweater, if you insist on wearing it. And it gives the guy a signal about you."

"Signal? What do you mean?"

"Look, Alice," Olivia said patiently, "no guy is going to hit on you when you wear a cutesy blue sweater."

After Olivia went off, clutching her cell phone, I put on the pearls. No point in the locket. It was too early in my friendship with Kevin to wear it.

The phone rang.

"Alice," called my mom. "It's for you."

"Hi," Kevin said. "It's me, Kevin."

"Hi, Kevin."

"Listen, Alice, I was thinking. It's early, not even noon, and if you're not busy, maybe we could go earlier and have lunch in the aquarium. I mean, if you're busy, we can go later, but I'm, well, I finished the book, so it would give us a chance to talk about it."

"Oh, great," I told him. "I'm free. I mean, I should be rereading the book, and getting my report done, but I have over a week, so sure, I'd love to . . . hear what you have to say."

"I'll be over in ten minutes," Kevin said.

I took a quick look in the mirror, and liked what I saw. Too bad I had to put my winter jacket on.

I raced downstairs and told Mom I was going out for lunch with Kevin.

"Do you have enough money?" she asked.

"Money?"

"To pay for your lunch. Nowadays, girls pay their way," said my mother. "Even when I was young, I always insisted on paying my way. Otherwise, the boy can get some ideas about the kind of girl you are. Here, take ten dollars. That should be plenty."

As far as I was concerned, any boy who is passionate about fish eyes wasn't somebody I had to worry about.

When the doorbell rang, I answered it without having my jacket on. I wanted Kevin to see me in my new sweater.

"Hi, Alice," Kevin said. "You look nice."

"So do you."

"Well, it's this shirt my mom gave me for Christmas. It's blue, and I don't know—"

"Kevin," I said, "you have blue eyes."

"Everybody has blue eyes in my family," Kevin said almost apologetically.

"Alice," Mom yelled from the kitchen. "Do you have the door open? It's freezing in here. Either come in or go out."

She came out of the kitchen, and smiled when she saw it was Kevin.

"Good morning, Kevin," she said.

"Oh, good morning, Mrs. Burns."

"Alice tells me you're interested in fish eyes," Mom added.

I grabbed my jacket, put it on slowly while Kevin made a feeble gesture as if he were trying to help me.

Once we were outside and walking toward the bus, I asked, "Well, what did you think of the book?"

Kevin made a face. "I'm sorry, Alice, but I really liked it. I know how you feel about Mary, but I guess Jane Austen is using her to make us all laugh. Elizabeth, she's the special one. She's so smart, so interesting—and the way she handles Darcy is just so right. You almost forget that this book is nearly two hundred years old."

"I'm changing Mary," I told him as we boarded the bus.

"You're *what?*"

"Well, I'm just making her a different person. She says such stupid things. So now I'm working on it. I got her to stop playing the piano at Netherfield, and now I'm working on having her shut up."

Kevin laughed. "You mean you're rewriting the book. Do you think Ms. Herran will go for it?"

The lady in the hooded raincoat was sitting in one of the front seats, the ones reserved for the handicapped or the elderly. Two hundred years is pretty old, I figured. She had a right to sit there.

"I'm not so worried about Ms. Herran," I told him as we settled down in the back.

"She'll probably think it's pretty original," he said. "And if you write it, I'm sure she'll approve."

"She did give me a C+."

But Kevin wasn't listening. He seemed to be having trouble with his arm. It kept wiggling around until he finally stretched it jerkily across the back of my seat.

I forgot about *Pride and Prejudice*. I forgot about the lady in the hooded raincoat. All I could think of was Kevin's arm around the back of my seat. I could see the embarrassment on his face as he pretended to look out the window. I wasn't Mary. I didn't have to shut up. "Kevin," I said, "now I think we should talk about those blind fish who swim in caves."

CHAPTER 11

I can't remember a meal I've ever eaten in my life that I enjoyed more than my lunch with Kevin in the cafeteria of the aquarium. Of course, I'd been there before with my family. Mom always complained about the grease, Olivia about the limited menu, and Rosie about having to come to the aquarium in the first place. Only the boys enjoyed the food.

But today, across the table from Kevin, I lingered over my slice of pizza.

Kevin had resumed talking about *Pride and Prejudice.* "I didn't think I was going to like it," Kevin said. "But I really hated when it ended. I might even read another one of her books. My sister says *Emma* is really the best, but since I'm just starting out, she recommends *Sense and Sensibility.*"

"Not me," I told him. "I don't enjoy the book. It's too much work for me getting Mary straightened out. A few parts are okay." I was thinking of Kevin in his scarlet coat, but I was responsible for that—not Jane Austen.

"I was wondering," Kevin said, pouring more ketchup over his french fries, "well . . . you're probably too busy, but . . . my friend, Jeff Lyons . . ."

"Jeff Lyons," I said. "I know him. He's . . ." I was about to say he was a nerd. He was a little, skinny guy with a worried look. He was in my P.E. class and was even more awkward than I am. Anytime I went to the library, I could count on seeing him, hanging over a pile of books.

"He's smart," I said. "I've known him about as long as I've known you."

"He's a genius," Kevin said respectfully. "He's going into physics—*astro*physics. I don't know anybody like him."

"Hmm!" I nodded. I didn't know anybody like him either.

"Well, his girlfriend, Maggie Deshaderavian, is giving a New Year's Eve party, and—"

"Jeff has a girlfriend?" I said. "A girlfriend!"

"She goes to another school. He met her a few months ago." Kevin laughed. "She's a jock. Plays basketball, and doesn't know anything about physics. She laughs a lot. She thinks Jeff is . . . well, she says he's cute. Anyway, she's giving a party, and I wondered . . . well, if you wanted to go . . . I mean . . . with me."

I put down the remains of my pizza and looked at Kevin's face. He was blushing. I don't think I'd seen anybody—girl or boy—blush. Although, in many books, especially this one by Jane Austen, women are always blushing. Kevin was definitely blushing—all across his face, even his ears.

He put down the ketchup without looking at me. "It's okay," he mumbled, "if . . ."

I put out my hand across the table and rested it on top of Kevin's hand, the one that had held the ketchup. "Kevin," I said, "I'd really love to go—especially with you."

There was more magic in that day. And I learned so much about fish and fish eyes. Kevin's hesitancy vanished as he led me from exhibit to exhibit, and talked about the varieties of fish and how they differed from one another. In the oceans, fish are hard to see because they are a metallic blue-green color, and they are streamlined so they can get away if they're pursued. Fish that live near the bottom are colored like mud, as camouflage.

Kevin was particularly eloquent on fish eyes. I learned,

among other facts, that there is a type of fish in South America that swims near the surface of the water and has four eyes so it can see above the water and below it.

Later, we walked hand in hand through the botanical gardens in Golden Gate Park. Nothing was blooming and the wind blew hard against our faces, but to me, it felt like the Garden of Eden.

"When did you first notice me?" I asked Kevin.

"Oh, Alice, I've always noticed you."

"I mean, when did you start liking me?"

"I guess last year when you fell down the stairs, and all the kids started laughing. I wanted to run and help you, but you stood up all by yourself and yelled 'Drop dead!' You were so feisty, and your eyes were so shiny. After that, I just couldn't help watching you. What about you?"

We were swinging our hands back and forth to keep them warm. I had borrowed Olivia's pink-and-white gloves and given Kevin one to wear while I wore the other one. The hands without the gloves were in our pockets.

"When did you first notice me?"

"In Macy's."

"Not before?"

I could see he was a little disappointed.

"Well, of course I noticed you before, and I knew you were very smart, but it wasn't until Macy's that I knew you liked me, and it was okay for me to like you."

Later, at home, I looked at the calendar. Less than a week before the vacation ended. I had to finish the book and write a report. All I wanted to do was sit very still and think about Kevin, but now time was growing short.

Page 205. The regiment is moving to Brighton, and Lydia has been invited by the colonel's wife to come along for a visit. Elizabeth tries to convince her father not to let Lydia go. She represents to him the lack of restraint and the impropriety of Lydia's behavior. If he allows her to go, Elizabeth says, *". . . she will, at sixteen, be the most determined flirt that ever made herself and her family ridiculous."*

Her father reassures her, saying nothing serious can possibly happen, and ends by remarking, *"At any rate, she cannot grow many degrees worse, without authorizing us to lock her up for the rest of her life."*

In the course of his comments, he says that Elizabeth has *"a couple of—or I may say, three very silly sisters."*

Of course, he is including Mary in his comment, along with Lydia and Kitty. I shake my head. It's becoming harder and harder for me to champion Mary if I follow the story as written.

So, I make my move. After Elizabeth leaves her father's study, a letter is delivered to him. He opens it, and reads.

My dear Sir,

Please forgive the impropriety of this letter. I should have spoken to you in person but that proved impossible. I had planned on doing so before the regiment left Meryton, but was suddenly ordered by Colonel Forster to leave earlier than my fellow officers in order to oversee the living arrangements in Brighton.

Perhaps your daughter, Miss Mary Bennet, has given you some indication of my sentiments. Perhaps not, since she has such a developed sense of delicacy. But I must assure you, dear Sir, that my regard for your daughter emboldens me to ask for her hand in marriage.

As to my background, which it is, of course, your duty to ascertain, I am the youngest son of the Earl of Harewood. My father has settled on me, 50,000 pounds and a small estate, which can be easily refurbished as my future wife desires. None of my fellow officers are aware of my family connections.

I believe Miss Mary Bennet is aware of my feelings, and returns them. Will you let me know, Sir, if you approve, and if I may address her directly?

Your Obedient Servant,

Edward J. Denny

There, I thought, not a bad letter at all.

Mr. Bennet seems astonished. He takes off his glasses, cleans them, reads the letter again, and feels his head. Finally, he stands up, leaves his room, and returns with Mary, who is blushing the way Kevin did, all the way across her face, including her ears.

"No," Kevin says. "Don't put me in the book. "

"You're already in it," I tell him. Of course, he's wearing his scarlet uniform. "I guess you're so much in my mind, I can't stop even if I wanted to."

"But it's not fair to make fun of me," he insists, "or the way I blush. Forget about Mary blushing. Just leave Mr. Bennet alone with Mary, and the two of us can take a walk around the grounds. Here in the book, it's spring. We won't need gloves."

The two of us walk together in the little wilderness to one side of the estate. The sun is warm, flowers are blooming, and Kevin and I are holding hands, and soon he's laughing and so am I.

She's sitting there on a stone bench as we pass. She's tapping one foot and shaking a finger at me. Even on this warm spring day, she's wearing her hooded raincoat. Kevin's hand is so comfortable, I try to ignore her, and I do.

CHAPTER 12

Kevin called that evening, just to mention some facts he had neglected to tell me about fish in other parts of the world, he said. But I knew he just wanted to talk.

The conversation on fish lasted for just a few minutes, and then he said, "You know, Alice, I didn't really tell you the truth when I said I started liking you last year when you fell down the stairs."

"Oh?"

"It was really when I saw you in the cafeteria before that. You were sitting with your friends—Jenny Chu and her pretty cousin, Cindy."

"Pretty?" I said. "Cindy?"

"Anyway, you were laughing, and Jenny was shaking her head. But you looked . . . so . . . glowing. I think that's really the first time I liked you. But maybe it was that other time in math—oh, Alice, I think I've always liked you."

Could any of this be real?

"Oh, Kevin!" For a little while, I wasn't able to say anything else. But then I suddenly remembered what Kevin thought of Cindy.

"Do you really think Cindy is pretty?"

"Yes, she's pretty. Not that I . . . Alice . . . I never . . ."

"Well, she's a pain in the neck," I told him. "And I never thought she was pretty. And she's not my friend. Jenny is, and just because she's Jenny's cousin, Jenny is stuck with her because her mother makes her be nice to her."

"Well, I don't know either of them very well. Jenny was in

my English class once. I know she's smart but she doesn't seem very friendly."

"She's kind of shy. Oh, I was forgetting. Do you know a guy named Sean Murray?"

"Sean Murray? Why do you want to know about him? I hope you're not interested in *him*!"

"Of course not, Kevin. I'm only interested in you. I hope you know that."

"Well, I guess so, but he's such a stud. Girls hang all over him. And he's not a . . . not a . . . Why are you asking about him anyway?"

"This is a secret, Kevin. You can't say anything to anybody."

"Oh, sure."

"Well, my friend Jenny likes him, and she wondered if you knew him."

"Tell her I know him, and I think he's a jerk. You'd better tell Cindy that too. He's got a new girlfriend every week. She should be careful." .

"What do you mean?"

"She keeps following him after P.E., and talking to him in the hall. And I've seen him pawing her and . . . kind of . . . well, patting her . . . where he shouldn't. He does that to lots of girls, and maybe you should tell her he likes to boast about all the girls who fall for him. You should warn her. She's asking for trouble with a guy like him."

"I will tell her, and Jenny too."

"Good. But let's not waste time talking about him. Let's talk about . . ."

"Us," I said. And we did.

                    ◦◯◦

Next day, I phoned Jenny, and started by asking her about the movie she and Cindy had gone to see.

"It was crummy," she said. "And Cindy is crummy too."

"Well, I wanted to tell you what Kevin told me about Sean Murray."

"That's all she talked about," Jenny said angrily. "'Sean said this and Sean said that.' Even during the movie she didn't stop."

"Kevin said he's a jerk, and he said I should tell you and Cindy he's a stud, and he brags about all the girls who follow him around. And he said that Cindy should—"

"She's going out with him," Jenny said. "She knew I liked him, but behind my back, she got to know him, and now she says he's her boyfriend."

"Kevin says he has a new girlfriend every week, and he said he saw Cindy follow him after P.E., and that Sean put his hands all over her."

"Good! I'm going to tell her mother. She's so protective of Cindy. She's always on my case about looking after her, and now Cindy thinks she's so great. Just because her braces came off before mine."

"Jenny, what are you talking about?"

"Haven't you noticed? For God's sake, Alice, her braces came off last month. Don't you notice how she's always smiling. You could tell her your brother died, and she'd just keep smiling."

"I never looked at her teeth, but—"

"And Dr. Yamamoto, my orthodontist, he keeps promising that my braces are coming off 'next time,' always 'next time.' And Cindy and I started at the same time, and her teeth stuck all the way out. Oh, Alice, it's just not fair."

"Jenny," I said, "just forget about Cindy." I didn't tell her that Kevin thought Cindy was pretty.

"And I'm never going to have lunch with her ever again. I don't want to speak to her. Oh, Alice!"

"Should I come over to your house, Jenny? I'll stop reading my book. I have time."

"No, no! I don't want my mother to hear us. Maybe I can come over to your . . . or we can meet at the mall." She sounded close to tears.

"Okay, but stop being so upset. I'll meet you near See's Candy at about—what?"

"Right away," she said. "Like, two o'clock."

"You're my only friend," Jenny said. We were sitting upstairs in the food court, eating ice cream. She reached across the table and patted my hand.

"Oh, you have other friends, Jenny."

"No, I don't." Her eyes were puffy, and I noticed that her braces glinted whenever she opened her mouth. "I always had to hang out with Cindy, but now that's finished. I already told her she'd better find somebody else to hang out with."

"And what did she say?"

"Oh, she just said she was doing me a favor hanging out with me, and you too. But now, she has Sean Murray and his friends."

"Well, that's fine with me," I told Jenny. "I never really liked her, but she's your cousin so I had to put up with her."

"But now that you're going out with Kevin"—Jenny sniffed—"you'll probably want to hang out with him and his friends."

"You know something, Jenny?" I said. "I always was glad

you weren't in any of my classes, because I didn't want to compete with you for grades. I never want to compete with you over boys either. I'm glad you weren't ever interested in Kevin. He doesn't have anything to do with our friendship. And now that I'm not going to have to put up with Cindy, you'll see, we'll be even better friends."

Jenny nodded. "I'm glad you said that. I guess I've been feeling sorry for myself. But tell me again what Kevin said about Sean Murray."

I couldn't give *Pride and Prejudice* any credit, but by the time, Jenny and I parted, I had begun thinking that she and I might become best friends—*real* best friends.

"What are you wearing for New Year's Eve?" my mother inquired.

"I don't know," I told her. "I've never been to a New Year's Eve party. Maybe I should ask Olivia."

"Never mind Olivia. When she goes to a party, I have to stand in front of the door before she leaves and look her over. She thinks I don't know she's planning to wear a dress that's backless and doesn't have much in the front, either. You can be sure I'm not going to let her out of here before she puts on something decent."

"Maybe nobody's dressing up at Jeff's girlfriend's party," I said. "Maybe I can wear that pretty sweater you gave me and my jeans."

Mom looked at her watch. "Let's go shopping," she said. "There's a big sale at Macy's, and I guess you'll need shoes too. Jeremy and Joey are off with your dad, so this is a good time."

Macy's was crowded with after-Christmas shoppers.

"What size are you?" Mom asked.

"I don't know," I told her. "The last dress I bought was for graduation from middle school. I haven't worn it since."

"We'll try the petites. Here's the escalator. Don't trip."

"Mom, I'm not a baby."

In the petite department, Mom discussed all my dimensions with a helpful, elderly saleswoman. "This is her first New Year's Eve party with a boy, and she's really shy."

The saleswoman nodded kindly while I tried to hide

behind a rack of bathrobes. I could hear the two of them gabbing away and laughing. Why in the world did I let my mother come shopping with me?

"We have some really cute dresses this year that aren't that, you know, indecent. Let me show you what I mean."

"Alice!" my mother called as she followed the saleswoman. I kept my distance.

"Now, look at this one." The saleswoman held up a dress that looked like a shapeless nightgown. It had some fake embroidery across the top. "Isn't it sweet?"

"Oh, yes," said my mother. "And such a pretty green color. What do you think, Alice?"

"No!" I growled. "I hate it. Why don't you let me look around myself?"

"Alice, you're being very rude." Mom apologized to the saleswoman, who responded by describing the terrible manners of her granddaughter. Both of them got deep into the discussion, which allowed me to sneak away and move quickly through the racks of party clothes around us.

Some of the dresses were certainly backless and nearly frontless. Olivia would look great in any of them. But for me, clumpy little me . . . I passed the glittery sequined dresses with plunging necks, the straight, tight ones, the shimmery silver sleeveless ones, and felt a rising fit of panic. And that's when I found it—a wine-colored velveteen dress with a round neck and an A-line shape.

"Well, Nancy," my mother was saying as I approached, holding up the dress, "it's just not the same world it was when we were growing up."

"No, Julia, it isn't, and I was telling my son the other day . . . oh, here's your daughter, and just look. That's the exact dress I was planning to show you."

Her approval nearly shook my pleasure in the dress, but when I slipped it over my head, it actually fit. I spun around in front of the mirror and admired myself. The neckline was perfect, and I could wear my locket.

"Isn't it a little long?" my mother asked. "Don't girls wear shorter dresses?"

"Nowadays," the saleswoman said, "any length is fine, but I could show you a few that are shorter." She looked at me doubtfully. "This may be the right length for her, though."

"I like it, Mom," I said firmly. "This is the dress I want."

Mom and the saleswoman exchanged numbers and promised to get together.

"Such a nice person," Mom said happily as we rode down the escalator to the shoe department. "I haven't been shopping with any of you for so long. Olivia insists on going by herself, and Rosie never wears anything new." Mom sighed. "Let's get you a pair of shoes, and maybe we can even have lunch."

It took a while to agree on a pair of shoes. We both agreed that black would be the right color, but Mom thought I should wear pumps with a heel.

"I tried on a pair and wobbled when I walked."

"You'll get used to it," Mom said. "They look very pretty."

"But Mom, my feet are too wide, and it hurts. Why can't I wear flats?"

"They're not dressy enough," Mom said. "Maybe a platform shoe." Which is what we finally ended up with.

It was fun having lunch with Mom. She seemed almost giddy.

"I used to have lunch with my old friends in the band after

we left high school. And before I married Dad. We used to have so much fun."

"Well, why don't you get together with them now, Mom?"

"Most of them aren't around. Lila, she was very talented, is actually in Hollywood. She plays the trombone in a band there. Karen's up in Seattle. She's a teacher and has three kids. Amy, she was my best friend, and . . . I've lost touch with her."

Mom hardly ate her ham-and-cheese sandwich, she was so busy talking.

"Mom, why don't you and Dad ever go out to lunch or dinner?" I asked finally.

Mom shook her head. "No time. Either he's working all sorts of crazy hours, or when he's home, you know, he likes to relax and watch TV or coach the boys' soccer team."

"But don't you have any fun together?"

Mom shrugged. She took a bite out of her sandwich and chewed happily. "When you have five kids . . . ," she said. "And then, I don't have much time anyway."

Mom worked part-time as a receptionist in a dentist's office.

I suddenly looked at my mother—really looked. She was thinner than I was, but she had the same hazel eyes and brown hair, with just a little gray at the sides.

"Mom," I said, "we look alike."

Mom sipped her coffee and smiled. "Everybody says so. They think you and the boys look like me, and Olivia and Rosie look like Dad. You've heard that before."

I guess I had, but I never thought much about it. "Mom," I asked, "what are you and Dad doing New Year's Eve?"

"Oh, we never do anything. He might even have to work. There are always so many drunks out. But if not, we stay home with the kids. And the ones who go out—it was only Olivia and

Rosie we had to worry about before, but now, you'll be going out too. We like to be around if you need us."

Suddenly, I felt sorry for my mother. "Why don't we go shopping for you, Mom?" I asked her. "You never buy anything pretty for yourself. Dad gave you some pots and pans for Christmas, and none of us gave you anything special."

"Aren't you sweet, honey, but really, I don't need anything. Maybe a new bra, but I can get that another time."

"Can I go with you? Maybe we can shop for some pretty shirts or sweaters. You never wear dresses."

Mom reached over and patted my hand. "Alice, you're really growing up so much nicer than . . . I mean, you're getting really thoughtful."

"No, I'm not. I—"

Mom was looking around the food court and interrupted. "Shopping is so much fun. Just look at all the people here enjoying themselves."

Not all. *She* was drinking tea and glaring at me out of as much of her face as I could see.

"I guess I should get home," I told Mom, jumping up. "I really have to finish that book and write my report before the vacation ends. I never thought I'd be so busy."

"It's good that you're busy," Mom said approvingly. "It's time you had fun instead of studying all the time."

Page 240. Nothing much happening there. So I can get back to Mary.

Mrs. Bennet is beside herself with joy. Mary will be the first of her five daughters married. "And such a handsome man, and just fancy, the son of an earl."

Mary smiles modestly.

"You'll need some new clothes," says Mrs. Bennet. "Denny will be coming here soon on a leave, and he will want you to meet his family. Oh, Mary, I'm so happy for you. You've worked so hard. It's time you had some fun."

That takes care of Mary for the time being. I returned to the actual book, relieved not to be burdened by Mary. To my surprise, I found myself totally immersed in the story, and enjoying Elizabeth Bennet's gradual change in feelings toward Mr. Darcy on her trip to Derbyshire.

Unfortunately, Lydia elopes with Mr. Wickham, and the whole Bennet family is overwhelmed. Mary returns to the story on page 255, and before I can stop her, she delivers one of her usual pompous remarks.

"Unhappy as the event must be for Lydia, we may draw from it this useful lesson; that loss of virtue in a female is irretrievable—that one false step involves her in endless ruin—that her reputation is no less brittle than it is beautiful—and that she cannot be too much guarded in her behaviour towards the undeserving of the other sex."

I closed the book and considered. There is only one thing I can do: remove Mary from the story completely until the end. Perhaps I can have her visit Denny's family, where she will remain until the book is finally completed. Or, she could die— no, that would make it too much like *Little Women*. I'll send her on a long visit to Denny's family, and let her come back for Elizabeth's and Jane's weddings. Maybe I could have her and Denny get married at the same time.

I had some decisions to make, but the phone rang and I hurried to answer it. I had a feeling it would be Kevin, and it was. Since Olivia now had her own cell phone, we were able to talk for a long time

Later, I thought about my parents. In a way, they reminded me of Mr. and Mrs. Bennet in *Pride and Prejudice*. Not that my mom is silly like Mrs. Bennet, or my dad makes fun of her the way Mr. Bennet makes fun of his wife. But it made me think about what having kids does to romance.

A framed photograph of them in the living room when they married showed a young, pretty, dark-haired woman dressed in a lovely white gown, looking up adoringly at a slim, tall, handsome fair-headed man who was smiling down at her. Now my father was bald, and his belly hung over his pants. Neither of my parents spent much time together except for visiting family members or coping with us kids.

Dad was watching TV, so I waited for a commercial to ask him, "Dad, how come you never take Mom out for lunch or dinner?"

"What?" My father looked at me, startled.

"I mean, she works so hard—you do, too—but how come you never take her out just by herself?"

The football game came on again. It was the last quarter, and my father dissolved into the TV set.

I went upstairs and opened *Pride and Prejudice*.

Page 282. Lydia marries Wickham in London, and Elizabeth discovers that Darcy's intervention (and money) brought it about. Otherwise, Wickham would have deserted Lydia.

Loud stamping and cheers erupted downstairs. Evidently the '49ers had won.

I resumed reading. To my astonishment and relief, Jane Austen leaves Mary entirely out of this part of the story. I begin relaxing and enjoying myself. Mrs. Bennet is filled with hope. Now that she has one daughter married (and one engaged, if we count Mary), she can focus on Jane.

Somebody tapped at the door. I roused myself. "Come in," I said.

Dad stuck his head around the door. "I was looking for you, Alice."

"They won, didn't they?" I asked, still holding the book in my lap.

"Great game! Great game!" Dad said. "Can I talk to you?"

"Sure." I put the book down, and Dad eased himself slowly into the wooden desk chair.

"Alice," Dad said, frowning, "why did you ask me about taking Mom out? Did she say anything to you?"

"Oh, no. It's just when we went shopping for me, for a dress for my New Year's Eve party, we had lunch, and she . . . she . . . well, she had such a good time, I thought you and she should go out sometimes."

Dad nodded. "We used to, before all of you were born. Even when Rosie was born, when she was little. But when she got older, she would run all over the place, and then the rest of you came along. . . ." His voice trailed off.

"Well, Dad, one of us older kids could watch the boys, and you two could go out. I asked Mom about New Year's Eve, and—"

"I'm working New Year's Eve," Dad said. "And if I wasn't, we'd both be home."

"I know. That's what Mom said. If you want to go out

Friday or Saturday, I'll watch the boys. I often do when Mom has to go shopping."

"I'm working Saturday," Dad said. "I'm off Sunday."

"So you can go Sunday."

"But where?" Dad asked.

"Take her out to a nice restaurant. Maybe Olivia knows one. But take her someplace where she can dress up, and you too."

Dad stayed quiet. He looked unhappy.

I reached out and put an arm around his shoulder. "You're a great guy, Dad, don't think you aren't. You're such a good father, we can always count on you, and you put up with all of us. And I know you and Mom love each other very much. Please don't feel bad."

"She was such a pretty girl," he said dreamily. "When I first met her, she was engaged to somebody else who had also played the trumpet in her high school band. I think he finally married one of her friends."

"Was it Amy?"

"Maybe, but how did you know?"

"That's the one she said she had lost touch with."

"When did she tell you that?"

"Today, when we had lunch at the mall."

Dad smiled. "That guy was pretty cut up when your mother broke the engagement. I remember he kept calling her and calling her. She, and I guess it was Amy, quarreled, but it all worked out for the best. Anyway, you're right. Maybe we should go out someplace nice. There used to be a restaurant in Sausalito with a great view. I'm pretty sure it's still there."

"But what about the food?"

My father shook his head. "Who cares about the food?

Food is food. It used to be the most glamorous place around. I took Mom there when we were first engaged, and she loved it. I'll go ask her." He jumped up from the chair.

"But, Dad," I warned, "don't say it was my idea."

"Of course not," he said. "What do you think I am? Stupid?"

I called Kevin and told him.

"You really are something," he said. "I wonder . . ."

"Wonder what?"

"Well, my parents hardly ever go out, either. Sometimes, I'm not even sure they like each other. They argue a lot in their bedroom when they don't think my sister and I are listening. I don't think it would do any good if I suggested that they go out."

"Mr. and Mrs. Bennet in *Pride and Prejudice* are such a dreary couple. They never do anything together. But my Dad really loved the idea, and I felt as if I had accomplished something."

"So you can thank *Pride and Prejudice* for that," Kevin said.

"I can thank it for a lot, I guess," I said. "If it weren't for *Pride and Prejudice*, you and I would never have gotten together."

"Oh, I don't know about that," Kevin said. "Sooner or later, I would have thought of something."

"Sooner or later? Like in five or ten years?"

"I'm not that slow," Kevin said. "Am I, Alice?"

We were laughing and yakking away until Jeremy appeared in the doorway making faces at me. "Alice, Joey is such a pest. I want to call Ben and play with him by myself tomorrow."

"Right. Okay, Kevin. I'll talk to you tomorrow."

"How about coming with me to the library?" he asked. "I

want to take out another book by Jane Austen—*Sense and Sensibility*. That's the one my sister recommended."

"Alice, please!"

"Ill be off in a minute," I said to Jeremy. "Great!" I said to Kevin.

Mom was standing in my room, looking at herself in the mirror and smiling. "Alice," she said as soon as I came in, "I have to go shopping tomorrow. Can you come?"

I knew why she had to go shopping, but I asked innocently, "Why, Mom?"

"You know why," she said, and before I could say, "No, I don't," she went on, still smiling at herself. "It's okay, Alice. You don't have to lie. I don't mind at all. Can you come tomorrow morning?"

"Uh, sure, Mom." I'd have to call Kevin and make our date later in the afternoon.

Mom was still looking in the mirror. "Maybe a black dress with sequins," she said.

"That sounds nice," I agreed.

"And short."

"Mom!"

"And shoes with high heels."

Mr. Bennet would never approve, I thought, but I had a feeling Dad would.

CHAPTER 15

Jenny and I began IMing each other. We talked about her report in Euro, and my new attitude toward *Pride and Prejudice.* We wrote about other things as well, and for the first time in our friendship, she asked me to come over to her house for lunch on December 30.

This time, I called her. "I'd love to," I said, "but I thought you didn't want your mother to hear anything personal."

"She won't be home," Jenny said. "And besides, she knows everything about Cindy, and she's even more upset than I am."

"Did you tell her?"

"No, Cindy did, and she told her mother too. Both of them are horrified."

Jenny laughed. "Now my mom doesn't want me to hang out with her. She thinks Cindy would be a bad influence on me."

"Should I bring anything?"

"No. Just come."

Jenny's house was a lot neater than mine. She and her younger sister each had a desk in the bedroom they shared. There were no other kids in the family.

"I never use a desk," Jenny said. "I always like to work at the kitchen table. My mom keeps saying that she never had a desk as a kid, but I like to work near people."

"Not me," I told her. "Maybe it's because there are five of us at home, so I work in the room I share with Olivia. There's only one desk there, but Olivia never uses it. I can't understand how she passes anything. She never seems to do any homework. At least Rosie is one of the best musicians in her school band."

I followed Jenny into the neat, pretty kitchen with no pile of unwashed dishes in the sink. She opened the refrigerator and peered inside. "What would you like, Alice?" she asked. "Cheese, peanut butter, or leftover chicken?"

"Chicken sounds good," I said. "Here, let me help."

It felt good, making sandwiches in a quiet kitchen with no other people to worry about. I cut up some carrots and tomatoes while she laid chicken slices on whole wheat bread.

The plates—blue-and-white—matched, and there were blue glasses for milk. At our house, most of the dishes didn't match.

Soon the two of us sat facing each other across the kitchen table. For just a moment, I felt shy, as if this were the first time we had ever eaten lunch all by ourselves.

"Maybe you can come over to my house for lunch," I said. "I'd invite you for a sleepover, but there's not much room at my house, unless you're willing to sleep in the living room. We could put sleeping bags on the rug."

Jenny nodded. "I'd like that. I've only slept over at Cindy's, and that was a long time ago. She's an only child, so she's got plenty of room."

"Maybe we can plan something in a week or so, after school starts. The vacation is just about over."

Jenny took a bite of her sandwich. "Are you . . . are you excited about going out with Kevin for New Year's Eve?"

"Well, yes, I am, but nervous too, because it's the first time, and I'm not sure about this party we're going to. I don't think I'll know any of the kids, except for Jeff."

Jenny chewed her sandwich and tried to look cheerful. If I could only bring her along! I knew she'd be sitting home with her family, maybe watching TV, and I decided to change the subject, but then Jenny said, looking down at a piece of chicken that had fallen out of her sandwich, "What's it like— I mean, having a boyfriend?"

"It's nice. I mean Kevin is such a good guy, it's more like having a friend, only he's a boy."

Jenny picked up the piece of chicken and stuck it back in her sandwich.

"I keep trying to think about how I would feel going out with a boy, but . . ."

"Jenny, it will happen to you the way it did with me."

Jenny shook her head. "No, that's not what I mean. It's just, I feel different when I'm near a boy—I get this funny feeling, and I'm not sure it's normal or not."

"Well, I feel the same way, and I never know who to talk to about it. My sister Olivia, I guess she's pretty experienced, and she keeps trying to talk to me about birth control."

"Birth control?"

'Well, to tell you the truth, Jenny, I looked it up on the computer because I wanted to know what kind of birth control people used—or maybe didn't use—in the nineteenth century. I was reading *Pride and Prejudice*, and I just wondered. So, Olivia happened to look over my shoulder, and she thought I was interested in birth control for myself."

Jenny swallowed the last bite of her sandwich and looked away. "I know they give condoms out at school, but usually . . . I realize it's the woman or girl who has to worry about it. Don't tell anybody, Alice, but I've been thinking I'd like to go get one, just to see what it looks like." She made a face. "Of course, I don't think I'll ever work up enough courage."

"In the nineteenth century," I told her, "they had condoms made of sheep's intestines."

"Yuck! I'm glad I didn't live then," Jenny said

"You know, camel drivers in desert countries used to put stones into female camels' uteruses if they were planning a long trip and—" But then Jenny starting laughing, and suddenly the two of us were off, talking and laughing, at the same time.

It was so easy talking to Jenny. It had never occurred to me that she would turn out to be the perfect person to talk to. We talked and laughed about when and how we would find out what sex was all about. We forgot about the jar of cookies on the table, and wondered which of us would be the first.

"You!" Jenny laughed. "Because you've got a boyfriend."

"No," I giggled, "because he's more interested in fish, and you probably will get involved with some sexy guy like Sean Murray."

That's when Jenny's mother came in.

"Hello there, Alice," Mrs. Chu said, smiling approvingly. "It's a great idea that the two of you decided to study together." She looked at the jar of cookies on the table.

"Jenny," she said, "why don't you put the cookies on a plate? Nobody wants to eat them from a jar."

Jenny mumbled something, got up, and arranged some cookies on a pretty blue plate. I had to keep my eyes averted from her face so I wouldn't laugh.

Nancy, the saleswoman, was working the next morning at Macy's. She and Mom exchanged greetings, and Mom told her how Dad was taking her out to a fancy restaurant in Sausalito. Nancy was delighted, and the two of them agreed that men never seemed to understand how little it takes to make a wife happy. Nancy was launching off into a long, boring complaint about how her husband never remembers her birthday, and Mom stood there shaking her head and making *tsk-tsk* sounds.

"Mom," I said finally. "We really need to start shopping. I'm supposed to meet . . . a friend at three."

"Her boyfriend," Mom explained, and told Nancy how I'd never gone out with a boy before.

Desperately, I grabbed the first dress I could reach from the rack and held it up. "How about this one, Mom?" I cried.

Mom sucked in her breath. "Oh no, Alice. I want something a little more . . ."

"I know just what you mean." Nancy smiled. "Here, let me show you a few I think are gorgeous."

Mom picked a sequined dark blue dress with a straight skirt. The hemline came a few inches above her knee.

"Too short," I said. "If you sit down in that dress, it's going to slide all the way up your legs."

Mom sat down, and sure enough, the dress moved all the way up her legs.

"I guess not," she said sadly. "If I was younger . . ."

Finally, she settled on a black dress with short sleeves and a fairly plunging neckline. It had sequins on top and a full, swirly skirt that came to her knees. When she sat down, it didn't move up her legs.

In the shoe department, she found high-heeled black sandals, and again we had lunch in the mall. Mom had invited Nancy to join us, but fortunately for me, she couldn't take a lunch hour until later.

It wasn't until three thirty that I finally met Kevin at the library.

"My mom is like a kid," I told him. "She couldn't stop oohing and aahing at everything she saw in the store. She didn't spend a lot of money, but she kept stopping to smell perfumes, try lipstick samples, and listen to some nutty woman who was demonstrating how to tie scarves."

Kevin was looking at the A's under fiction. ". . . Andersen . . . Atwater . . . here . . . Austen. Now, just look at how many *Pride and Prejudice*s they have. Ah . . . here's *Sense and Sensibility*. I hope it's as good."

There she was, sitting at a library table, smiling and nodding at Kevin, not me. The hooded raincoat still covered most of her face.

"I wonder what Jane Austen looked like," Kevin said, flipping through the pages. "My sister says the only portrait they have of her is a little drawing her sister did. She looks crabby and not very pretty. Eleanor says she's positive Jane Austen looked a lot better than that."

"Well, maybe it's better nobody knows exactly what she looked like," I said. "It's more of a mystery that way, isn't it?"

She had turned away as I said that. All I could see now was the back of her head.

It was raining, so we sat in a quiet corner of the library and spoke in low voices.

"What are you wearing to the party?" I asked Kevin.

"Oh, nothing special. My jeans and a sweater, I guess. What about you?"

"Well . . . my mom thought . . . I mean, I guess, I bought a dress and shoes."

"You did?"

"I don't have to wear them. If you're going in jeans, maybe I should too."

Kevin wrinkled up his face thoughtfully. "I do have a jacket and a dress shirt. When my grandmother died, my mom made me dress up for the funeral. I don't know what anyone else is wearing. As a matter of fact, I don't even know who's coming. I just know Jeff and Maggie, his girlfriend. I don't really know her very well. But Jeff does, and he's my best friend."

"I've never been to a New Year's Eve party," I confessed. "Usually, I'm home with my parents and my brothers. They like to make a lot of noise at midnight, bang pots and pans together, and stomp around. My mom lets them stay up late to watch TV."

"Well, I've never been to a New Year's Eve party either," Kevin admitted. "Maybe I'll call Jeff and find out what he's wearing."

I felt relieved. "Great, and then let me know. I don't have to wear the dress. I can always save it for some other occasion." There didn't seem to be too many occasions other than Christmas dinner at my grandparents' house, or maybe if somebody died.

"I never went to a funeral," I told Kevin. "What was it like when your grandmother died?"

"It was hard to believe," Kevin said. "I liked her a lot. Most of our family cried—me too. She was my mom's mother, and my mom and her sisters cried, but very quietly. There was a distant cousin of theirs who made most of the noise—crying and screaming. It was almost funny since she and my grandmother hardly ever met. After the funeral, we all went back to one of my aunts' house, and that cousin ate more than anybody else. There was so much food. People laughed and joked, you'd never think anybody had died. Anyway, look, it's not raining anymore."

"Good," I said. "I need to get home and finish the book. I don't have even a week left."

"I'll walk you home. Then I'll call Jeff, and let you know."

Page 307. Mr. Bingley has finally proposed to Jane, to the great joy of Mrs. Bennet and the delight of all the family. Mary is mentioned from time to time here, but does not speak and is generally ignored. Perhaps I can safely bring her back now from visiting Denny's family.

The book is coming to an end, and suddenly, I don't want it to end. With Mary out of the way, I'm enjoying it so much, I want to keep reading it and reading it.

Page 325, is the most important chapter in the book. Darcy is going to propose to Elizabeth, and she is going to accept him. No, no! Not yet!

I closed the book. How in the world was I going to finish this masterpiece (now that I'd dealt with Mary) and spend my whole life reading inferior books? And what kind of a report would I write? Then it came to me. I couldn't write a report if I changed the story as Jane Austen wrote it. I couldn't claim the book is a masterpiece if I changed it. I would have to respect the author's wishes and leave Mary as she is—a pompous nerd readers laugh at. The book had changed my life, had changed Kevin's, and, hopefully, Mom and Dad's. Was it right to change Mary if she made no attempt to change herself? Who was I to dare to decide her future?

Olivia came into the room, pouting. "As soon as I can, I'm moving out of this place," she said.

"Why, Olivia? What happened?"

"Mom's impossible. She says I can't wear my new dress to the New Year's Eve party."

"Oh, Olivia, I wanted to ask you—"

"She's so bossy. I told her I'm seventeen. She should see what some of the other girls wear."

"Well, that's what I wanted to ask you, Olivia. Do all the girls dress up for a New Year's Eve party? And how about the boys?"

"Oh, boys!" Olivia shrugged. "Who cares what the boys wear. Some of them even wear jeans. But girls want to dress up." She looked me over for a moment and continued, "Now your dress . . . well, it's kind of sweet. But then you're young so . . ."

"You're only a year and a half older than me."

"Alice!" Olivia said, shaking her hair. "I'm older, not only in years, but in experience. Anyway, I'm going to tell Mom, if she doesn't let me wear that dress, I'll . . ."

But she was out the door before finishing her sentence.

When Kevin called later that evening, he said, "I don't know, Alice. Jeff isn't sure what to wear, and he said Maggie told him not to worry about it. He could wear anything he liked, even jeans."

"It's okay, Kevin," I told him. "My sister Olivia said girls dress up but boys don't have to."

"Why is that?"

"It doesn't make much sense, does it?" I said. "Maybe girls like to dress up, and most boys don't."

"Do you like to dress up?"

I thought about my new dress and the sweater Mom gave me for Christmas. "I don't know," I told him. "It's all kind of new for me. Anyway, let's just dress the way we like. I'll wear my new dress and shoes. You don't have to wear the clothes you wore to your grandmother's funeral. That wouldn't make you feel happy."

Olivia spent most of the evening arguing with my mother. It gave me the opportunity to have our room to myself. At a quarter to ten, I closed the book.

Olivia came storming into the room at five of ten.

"You're crying," she said. "I hope you're not upset because Mom is being so horrible to me."

She sat down next to me on my bed and put her arms around me. "Never mind, Alice, never mind. She'll give in. She always does. Don't cry."

I didn't tell her why I was crying. She wouldn't understand. So I settled myself comfortably under her arm, and let her fuss over me and comfort me. I needed it. I had finished the book.

Mom insisted that Kevin show up at home before we left for the party.

She stood there like the wife of a policeman while Kevin, the criminal, stood before her, squirming.

He looked great, I thought—his hair brushed back, his face squeaky clean, and his clothes a satisfactory compromise. Under his sweater, I could see the top of a button-down shirt, and his pants were tan chinos with a crease down the center of each leg.

"I want Alice home before one," commanded my mother.

"Mom!" I protested. "You let Olivia and Rosie stay out later."

Mom held up her hand. "And Kevin, I want you to promise that you won't drink any alcoholic beverage or take drugs."

"Oh, yes," Kevin said fervently. "I promise. I never do."

"And if anybody else at the party is drinking or taking drugs, I want you to promise that you will call me immediately."

"I promise."

"And, Kevin, I also want to make sure that you won't take a ride in anybody's car, whether they're drinking or not."

"Remember me, Mom?" I said. "You sound like some kind of a sexist, only talking to him. What about me?"

"I know you, Alice," Mom said. "I can trust *you*. Now, Kevin, I don't want you riding around in some other kid's car."

"No," Kevin said, embarrassed. "We won't have to because—"

"I'm driving you over," Mom said, reaching for her jacket.

"And you can call me when you're ready to leave—before one—and I'll pick you up."

"Mrs. Burns," Kevin said, blushing, "my mother, well, she's outside. She . . . feels the same way you do, and she's insisting that she'll pick us up."

Mom nodded approvingly. "I'll go outside and speak to her. Maybe if she takes you one way, I can pick you up."

"This is so humiliating," I told Kevin. "I almost don't feel like going."

"It's okay, Alice," Kevin said. "Jeff's father is driving him to Maggie's house. I guess some of the other kids are being driven over by one of their parents too."

"Maybe in a year or two, they won't treat us as babies," I mumbled.

"Don't count on it." Kevin grinned. "You look very pretty, Alice. I don't think I've ever seen you in a dress before."

"You look nice too, Kevin."

He reached out and took my hand, just as Mom came rushing back into the room. Quickly, Kevin dropped it.

"Okay," she said cheerfully, "Mrs. Tanner will drive you there, and I'll pick you up. Remember to call before one. Have a good time, kids, but don't—"

"Okay, Mom," I said. "And don't worry. We'll obey all your commands."

We could hear loud music and laughter as we rang Maggie's bell. When she opened it, I thought maybe we'd come to the wrong place. Maggie's hair was dyed a bright blue. She had a snake tattoo on one of her arms, a bare midriff, and a short, short iridescent skirt.

"Maggie?" Kevin asked, retreating from the door.

"You must be Kevin." Maggie grinned. "And I guess you're . . ."

"Alice."

She looked me over and laughed. But she opened the door. "Come on in. We're down in the basement. My parents are pretty much confined to the kitchen. They won't bother us."

Kevin and I moved closer to each other as she led us down the stairs. It was dark down there, with different-colored candles on low tables. Some kids were dancing, while others were in dark recesses. Most of them were barely visible.

"Uh, where's Jeff?" Kevin asked.

"Oh, Jeff—he's such a party pooper." Maggie laughed. She laughed a lot. Almost every time she said something, she laughed. "Come over here. Maybe it will wake him up."

Bird brain, I thought.

We followed her to a small table against one of the walls. It had a candle in the middle, and Jeff was there, blinking and looking around nervously.

"Kevin!" he whispered joyfully. "I thought you'd never come."

"Okay, now your friends are here. So get up and let's dance."

"But, Maggie, I don't know how to dance."

"You'll learn," she said, laughing, yanking at his arm.

Kevin and I sat down, and watched him stumbling around with Maggie. She spun and gyrated until the two of them were lost in the darkness. From time to time, other couples appeared, and disappeared into the darkness.

"I don't know, Kevin," I said. "Some of them, what I can see of them, look very odd. See that one over there with a bandana around his . . . I think it's a . . . his . . . head. And see, his pants are so low, when he turns, they—oh, no!"

"Well, don't look at him, Alice. See, there's a girl in a silver fringy dress. She looks—I guess it's a *she*—almost normal."

The two of us huddled together until Maggie and Jeff returned. "Come on, both of you," Maggie laughed. "Get up and dance."

"I don't know how," I mumbled. Kevin echoed me in an even lower mumble.

"You can't be any worse than Jeff. Come on, get on your feet and watch me."

So Kevin and I stood up and tried to follow what Jeff and Maggie were doing. But the two of them disappeared among the other dancers. We could hear Maggie's laughter almost everywhere we moved. We started rocking back and forth, continually bumping into other couples.

"I think the idea," Kevin said, "is to just move any way you like. It doesn't really matter what you do. Besides, nobody is watching." He shuffled around and stumbled into another couple. I laughed, but stamped my feet, feeling the new shoes pinching my toes, and snapped my fingers above my head.

"It was a lot easier when we danced at the Netherfield Ball in *Pride and Prejudice*," I told him. "But that was more dignified, and the lights were on."

Suddenly, the door at the top of the basement stairs opened, and a woman's voice said, "Maggie! Don't you think it's too dark down here? Why don't you put some more lights on? We don't want anybody to fall down."

"Mom!" came Maggie's voice from out of the darkness. "Just stop it. Nobody's going to get hurt. Why don't you and Dad enjoy yourselves? You don't have to stay in the kitchen. You can go into the living room, or even go out."

"We'll be in the kitchen if you—if anybody—needs something," said Maggie's mom, closing the door.

More and more kids joined the party, and finally there was hardly any room to move around.

"Let's go sit down somewhere," Kevin said breathlessly, and tried to steer us back to our former table. But some other people were there, so we ended up sitting halfway up the stairs. Kids came running up and down, but nobody appeared to notice anyone else. Finally, Jeff joined us. "I've been look-ing all over for you," he panted. "I don't know anybody else here."

"What school does she go to?" I said.

"She goes to the School of Performing Arts. She's very gifted. She plays the violin, and is the concert mistress in her orchestra."

"She plays *what*?" I asked.

"The violin. I went to a concert there with my brother Sam. He plays the cello. She had a beautiful solo. And after-ward, he introduced us, and she . . . just seemed to like me. She's very smart—a straight-A student—and she's also on their basketball team. I don't know what she sees in me. She's sev-enteen, and I'm only—"

"Fifteen and a half," Kevin and I said at the same time.

"She has a license, and she wanted to pick me up, but my parents said no."

"She doesn't look like . . . well, I guess first impressions aren't always right," I said.

"No, they're not," came a voice from the darkness—a laughing voice—and Maggie emerged into the dim light. "That's right out of *Pride and Prejudice*. You know, Jane Austen wanted to call it that originally."

"You read?" I couldn't help asking.

Maggie laughed and sat down next to us. She had a nose ring, and a shiny hoop in one ear. "I've read all of Jane Austen's novels, and now I'm on a George Eliot kick. That *Middlemarch* is really cool."

"And you play the violin?" I asked incredulously.

Maggie chortled and shrugged her shoulders. "I can't help it. I'll probably end up doing it professionally. Come on, Jeff, get up. You'll wear out your bottom."

Many of the kids at the party, as we discovered later, also went to SOPA and played in the band or orchestra. But from what we could see, few of them looked like what musicians were supposed to look like. It was too dark to see what any of them were drinking or smoking, and from our perch on the stairs, we didn't look too hard.

Kevin kissed me. I kissed him.

"Are you Mary?" Kevin asked, pulling me closer.

"Not anymore." I stroked his face. "Tonight I'm Elizabeth."

"Then I'm Darcy," he said as midnight arrived. "Happy New Year, Elizabeth."

"Happy New Year, Darcy."

We were so busy kissing, I nearly missed her as she danced by, still in her hooded raincoat. It was too dark to see who she was dancing with, but she seemed to be having a good time. In the darkness, I almost thought I saw a smile on her face.

CHAPTER 18

I sat over the computer, thinking about how to begin my report. Thursday, January 1. I had four days to finish it, and didn't know what to say. Kevin was spending the day at his aunt and uncle's open house in Davis. He had invited me to come, but I declined. Aside from not enjoying other people's relatives, I had to get this paper done.

"*Rosie!*" my mother shouted.

No answer.

Rosie was practicing her trombone, so Mom had to shout louder.

Finally, Rosie yelled back. "What?"

"I need you to go to the store and get me a few things."

"Why don't you ask Alice?"

"Because she's busy doing her homework."

"Well, I'm practicing."

"*Rosie!*"

What a change, I thought. Another piece of the magic that surrounded me ever since *Pride and Prejudice* came into my life. This was the second time Mom had asked somebody else to go shopping. And suddenly, Mom and I had become closer.

Just this morning, she had asked me to look at the outfit she was going to wear on her big date with Dad Sunday night. The dress fit her tightly around the bust and she wobbled when she walked on the thin high heels of her new shoes.

"Well?" she asked hopefully. "What do you think?"

What did I think? A middle-aged woman, dressed like a

teenager. Her smile was sweet, and she had a new hairdo, but she looked her age.

"You look wonderful, Mom. Dad's going to be thrilled."

She turned to smile at herself in my mirror. "I don't think your father will even notice."

But Dad would notice, I knew, because last night, he'd shown me two ties, one blue and the other a striped red-and-white.

"What do you think, Alice?" he asked. "I'll wear a white shirt, and the gray suit I hardly ever wear. Should I get a new tie? What do you think?"

"Wear the blue one. It brings out the color in your eyes."

"She won't even notice," he said.

So there I sat, thinking about a book that had changed my life. I didn't think Ms. Herran would believe that because of *Pride and Prejudice*, in two weeks' time, I had a boyfriend, a new relationship with my sister Olivia, and the approval and confidence of my parents. I couldn't write that Mom and Dad seemed almost giddy with excitement over a single date after twenty years of marriage. Or that I had changed too. What could I say?

Well, I would have to admit that it was not a tragedy, and that Mary truly was a nerd. I also would have to admit that, even if you disagreed with a particular author's point of view, you had no right to change what she had written. You would simply have to write your own book.

By the time Kevin returned from his open house, I had worked six hours nonstop on the report. I was exhausted but relieved.

"I'm glad you're finished," he said when he called, "because I was hoping I could see you tomorrow."

"Kevin," I told him. "I've decided what I'm going to be."

"I think I can guess."

"What do you think?"

"A magician," he said.

"No, no. I'm going to be a writer."

"Well, that's magic too, isn't it? You wave your magic wand, and you create a whole new world."

"Kevin, I think you're great."

A short pause, and I imagined Kevin blushing. "So," he asked, "are you free tomorrow?"

"I need to make a few more changes on the paper—it's a long one, seventeen pages. But I could be free by lunch."

"I'll make us sandwiches," he suggested. "I like peanut butter and banana."

"It's freezing outside," I said. "You could come here for lunch."

"Uh-uh," Kevin said. "I mean, I respect your family and all that, but wouldn't it be more fun if we went up to Stow Lake and took out a boat? It's not that cold."

"Okay, but I'll make my own sandwich."

"My turn," Kevin insisted. "You have to finish your report. Do you think you'd like peanut butter and banana?"

"No, I don't think so. I really like cheese and ketchup."

"We're a good pair," Kevin said. "I think we were meant for each other. Now, get back to work. I'm glad you're nearly finished with your report."

He didn't offer to read my paper, but he did make a very good cheese-and-ketchup sandwich. We took out a pedal boat and ate our sandwiches as we moved twice around the cold gray lake. Our hands and fingers were stiff when we turned in the boat.

I didn't see her at all that day.

Both Mom and Dad looked nervous as they met each other in the living room before their big date. The whole family had assembled to witness the event.

"Now drive carefully," Rosie advised.

"And Dad, don't drink too much, or if you do, let Mom drive," Olivia added.

"And don't stay out too late," Joey chimed in. "We have to go to school tomorrow, and Mom has to be up early to make breakfast and our lunches."

Mom and Dad were smiling shyly at each other as they left.

"Have a good time," I called after them.

"Now what do we do?" Jeremy asked.

We all looked at each other.

"Mom left some chicken nuggets and frozen french fries," I said. "Why don't we go eat?"

It would be the first time the five of us had sat down to eat a meal at the same time without one parent or the other present.

"Are you going out tonight, Olivia?" Rosie asked.

"No. Are you?"

"Not tonight. Tomorrow we have to practice for the February concert at school. How about you, Alice? Are you going out with Kevin?"

"No, he's sick. We went boating on Stow Lake, and it was so cold, he's been sick ever since."

We finished heating up the chicken nuggets and the french fries. Olivia made a feeble effort at putting a salad together.

There was ice cream and leftover pecan pie in the freezer, and by the time we finished, all of us were happily talking and laughing together.

"Maybe we should do the dishes," Olivia suggested.

"You're right," I agreed. "We wouldn't want Mom and Dad to come home and find the kitchen a mess." Naturally, all of us were supposed to do certain chores, but none of them were ever accomplished without bitter objections.

It was amazing how all of us pitched in with continued good humor. When we were finished, the kitchen was clean, and Jeremy and Joey had made their own school lunches.

"That was fun," Joey said. "Hey, why don't all of us hang out together?"

"We could watch TV," Jeremy suggested.

"Maybe there's something else we could all do," I said.

It took some time before we could agree. Poker. For money. All of us hurried off to find spare change—pennies, nickels, and dimes. Only Jeremy was totally broke, so the rest of us loaned him fifty cents.

As the evening progressed, the piles of money shifted back and forth.

"Do you think this is legal?" Jeremy asked. "Would Dad have to arrest us if he found us gambling?"

"Nah!" Joey said.

Nobody argued. Nobody complained. All of us were completely focused on the game and on each other. When either Mom or Dad was home, somebody usually was complaining or making a fuss.

By eleven, Joey said he was too sleepy to play anymore. He also had the highest pile of money.

"Should one of us wait up for Mom and Dad?" Rosie asked.

But none of us did. We hugged and kissed one another and said what a great evening it had been.

The next morning, Mom was bustling around the kitchen, and Dad had left for work.

"Did you have a good time, Mom?" I asked.

"It was wonderful, Alice, but I'm so tired, I can hardly keep my eyes open." Mom yawned.

"You must have gotten in pretty late."

"I guess we did," Mom said, smiling, "but it was worth it. And just look at how neat the kitchen looks. I hope it wasn't too much work for the rest of you."

"Oh, no, Mom, we all worked together. It was—"

Rosie came storming into the kitchen. "Joey just broke my sunglasses, and tell Olivia to get out of the bathroom!"

Another day, and not a magical one.

CHAPTER 19

Kevin didn't make it back when school started again. I knew he wouldn't be coming, because I had tried to speak to him the night before.

"He has laryngitis," said his sister, Eleanor. "He wanted me to call you and say he won't be able to come to school tomorrow. He's running some temperature, and my mom wants him to stay home until it's normal."

"Oh!"

"Could you get his homework for him?" Eleanor asked.

"Sure, but—"

"She'll get your homework for you," Eleanor called out. "Kevin is sitting right here listening to me—oh, now he's writing something for me to tell you. In the meantime, I understand you ended up liking *Pride and Prejudice*."

"I loved it," I said passionately. "It's the best book I ever read."

Eleanor agreed. "I guess it is. *Emma* is pretty good too. It's hard to choose. Poor thing only wrote six novels and some odds and ends."

"Why is that?"

"She died young, at forty-one."

"That's not so young," I said. "My mother is forty-one."

"Well, it's kind of tantalizing wondering how many other books she might have written. Oh, here . . . Kevin wants me to tell you that Jeff called earlier today, and he couldn't talk to him. He wants you to tell Jeff that he's sick, and to thank him for inviting you both to the party."

"I'll tell him."

"Oh—wait! He's writing something else. Here it is. He says you should call him tomorrow after school. He thinks his voice will be better."

Ms. Herran accepted my paper and laid it on her desk. "I'll read it as soon as I can," she promised.

"Please read it soon," I urged. "It's completely the opposite of my first paper."

"I'm glad to hear that," she said vaguely. "Now, Brandon, stop showing off, and Lena, I want to see you later. Please, everybody, sit down, and we can start discussing our new project."

I sat down and looked around me, starting with Ms. Herran. Sure, she squinted and wore unfashionable glasses, but wasn't I lucky to have her as my teacher? She had introduced me to Jane Austen and helped me to understand what a great writer she is. Today, Ms. Herran was wearing a pretty green velour turtleneck and gray pants. In spite of the funny glasses, she was actually a pretty woman. Strange that I had never noticed before.

The pale winter sun came through the windows and highlighted Robin Heller's mousy brown hair. She must have felt me looking at her, and turned, smiling at me. I smiled back and felt a great sense of happiness flowing through me.

P.E. was never my favorite subject. But today, I was feeling so cheerful, I walked into the gym and nodded pleasantly to the teacher, Mrs. Schneider. She was playing a CD of something loud and fast.

"Please stand in two straight lines—girls on one side, boys over here. Today, we'll start this semester with some ballroom dancing."

"Hi, Alice," somebody muttered. It was Jeff Lyons, and I gasped when I looked at him.

"I'm breaking up with Maggie," he said, heading to stand in the boys' line.

Jeff's hair was dyed sort of a fuchsia, and he was wearing low-rise jeans. He looked so weird, I had to put my hand in front of my mouth so I wouldn't laugh out loud.

"Now, what I want," Mrs. Schneider said, "is for you all to practice these dance steps. Just watch me. And Frank Bloomberg, stop chewing gum."

Mrs. Schneider was a tall, large woman who looked exactly like a P.E. teacher should. The muscles on her arms bulged, and her voice boomed.

We all stamped around for a while as she moved up and down the rows, criticizing our moves. "Not enough energy, Louise. Come on Jeff, loosen up. . . ."

In my mind, even without the book in front of me, I found myself dancing at the Netherfield Ball. Only I wasn't dancing with Darcy. I was dancing with Kevin in his scarlet coat.

"I know I'm crazy," I said to him. "I've finished the book, but I can't let it go."

We circled each other, and he bowed while I curtsied.

"You're so graceful," he said. "And I do love that new dress you're wearing. Especially when you curtsey."

"Alice, I really don't know what you think you're doing. The rest of the girls in your line are moving the other way," Mrs. Schneider said.

"Oh. I'm sorry."

"Just try to keep your mind on what you're doing," she said harshly.

Afterward, she changed the music and announced that we were going to learn the waltz.

"Alice, will you dance with me? I want to explain what happened," Jeff asked.

I put my left arm on his shoulder, which was easy because he was shorter than I was, and he put his right arm carefully around me—high up above my waist. Both of us joined our other hands and tried to waltz in time with the music. Jeff was having trouble keeping his pants up, so from time to time, he had to drop my right hand to yank at his pants.

"She's made a fool of me," he said. "I told her yesterday, and she said I was hopeless anyway, and she didn't think I was fun anymore."

"So why are you wearing those pants if you broke up with her?"

We were stepping on each other's feet, and Mrs. Schneider moved over and tried to rearrange us. "Stand up straight, Jeff, and Alice, try to move a little more gracefully." Fortunately, a couple of kids kept bumping into other kids, and she hurried off to disentangle them.

"I can't find my regular pants or my gym suit—she's made me so crazy," Jeff said, yanking at his pants again. "Maybe they're in the wash. I'm going to throw these out as soon as I get home."

"Oh, you'll find your regular pants," I said. "Just be glad you're through with her. I didn't think she was your type anyway."

"No, she wasn't," he said, as we staggered around together. "But who is my type? The way I look, no girl would be interested in me."

"Well, you can rinse that color out of your hair, and if you can't, maybe you could cut it off, or even dye it."

MARILYN SACHS

"No more dye," he said bitterly. "Why didn't I say no? She's such a bossy girl, and I'm such a klutz."

"You're not a klutz any more than I am. I guess we just have to try to enjoy what we're doing."

"I suppose you're right."

"There!" I told him. "You haven't stepped on my feet, and I haven't stepped on yours."

"It's kind of fun, isn't it," he said. And then there we were, suddenly moving around in time with the music.

"Now, I want everybody to watch Jeff and Alice," Mrs. Schneider said. "Just look at how well they're dancing."

And we were—waltzing without bumping into anybody or stepping on each other's toes. Mrs. Schneider stood beaming at us while the other kids watched.

"See," I told him, "neither of us are klutzes."

Jeff laughed and grabbed me a little tighter, and a little lower toward my waist. "It's fun, Alice. I haven't enjoyed myself like this all weekend. Why can't I find a girl I can really have fun with?"

And it came to me as we whirled around the gym. "Well, my best friend, Jenny Chu, is a lot of fun."

Mrs. Schneider clapped her hands, and said, "Good! Good! Good!"

"Jenny Chu?" Jeff asked. "Is she the one with the pretty cousin?"

"Forget the cousin," I gasped. "Jenny's cousin is bossy and a lot like Maggie. Jenny would be a great girlfriend for you. You're Kevin's best friend, and Jenny's mine. And she's smart, and her mother bakes wonderful cookies."

"She wouldn't like a guy like me," Jeff gasped. We were really flying around the room now. "Would she?"

"Let me handle it," I told him.

The music stopped, and Mrs. Schneider came up to us, smiling and wagging her head back and forth.

"You see?" she said. "All of a sudden, the two of you—not exactly my most, well, promising students—are doing a wonderful waltz. I always say, if people make an effort, there is nothing they can't do."

Jeff yanked up his pants and said, "That was fun."

The bell rang, and as we hurried off, I said to Jeff, "Should I set something up with Jenny?"

"Sure," he answered. "But I hope she likes to dance."

CHAPTER 20

Jenny and I met down in the cafeteria, as usual, once lunch period started.

"Jenny," I said, "wait till I tell you what just happened with Jeff Lyons."

"Here!" she said, holding out a sandwich bag filled with cookies. "My mother wants me to give this to you."

"That's nice, but why?"

Jenny grinned. "She feels you have a good influence on me."

"It's a good thing she didn't hear what we were talking about. Mmm! These are delicious. Anyway, I have something to ask you."

"She's a good baker when she has the time," Jenny said, "and she really likes you. I didn't tell her about Kevin, but she's impressed with your grades."

"Well, yours are just as good."

"She's never satisfied, but—uh-oh, look who's heading our way."

"Hi, Jenny. Hi, Alice," Cindy said. She stood uncertainly at our table. "Can I sit here?"

"I thought you said you didn't want to sit with us anymore," Jenny snapped. "I thought you said you were going to hang out with Sean Murray and his pals. I thought—"

"He doesn't want me to," Cindy said tearfully.

"Oh, sure, Cindy, sit down," I said—the hardest thing I ever had to say. The return of Cindy meant the end of Jenny's and my new friendship. But how could I say no to somebody whose mouth was trembling and whose eyes were already filled with tears?

"You said we were losers, and you wanted to be with the popular kids. You said—"

Jenny evidently had a long list of *you said*s, but then Cindy interrupted and said bitterly, "I'm the biggest loser in the world."

"Where's your lunch?" I asked quickly.

"I forgot to bring it," she said. "And anyway, I'm not hungry."

". . . and the dentist took your braces off before he took mine off, and . . ." Jenny continued.

"Here," I said. "Take half of my sandwich. It's egg salad with olives."

"I don't like olives," she said.

"Well, you can pull them out. Here, I'll do it for you." I opened one half of the sandwich and began pulling out the olives.

"He said I was a nothing . . . and . . . some other words I wouldn't want to repeat. He said he would be ashamed to go out with a girl like me. He said I was fat and had a big nose."

"Listen," I told her, "my friend Kevin Tanner said he thought you were very pretty." Kevin had never said "very," but I could see Cindy needed all the help she could get. It was obvious even to Jenny that Sean Murray had dumped her. Jenny shut up.

"Kevin Tanner?" Cindy asked.

"He also said that Sean Murray is a jerk, and you should keep away from him. He said Sean brags about all the girls who fall for him, and he thought you should know that."

"Kevin Tanner said that?" Cindy began looking around the cafeteria.

"He's not in school today," I told her. "He has a cold."

"Kevin is Alice's boyfriend," Jenny explained quickly, "so leave him alone."

"He's nice," Cindy said, taking half of my sandwich and biting into it. "Mmm, this is good, and I'm really hungry."

"And there's cookies, too," I said. "Jenny's mother baked them."

"Oh, I love her cookies," Cindy said, "but she's angry at me, and so is my mom. She's grounding me for a couple of weeks. I keep telling her it's all over, but she won't listen. To be honest, it never really began. I thought he liked me. He acted as if he did, but it only went on a couple of days, and once, after school, in the football field . . ." She looked at me curiously. "Kevin Tanner is really your boyfriend?" I could feel her eyes roaming over my face and hair. She must have been wondering why any boy would be interested in a girl like me. My kind feelings for her began to dissolve.

"Yes, he really is," I said, and then concentrated on my half of the egg salad sandwich with olives.

"Here," Jenny said. "I'll share one half of my sandwich with the two of you so we'll each have the same amount, and Cindy, you can have some of my cookies too."

"You guys are great," Cindy said. "I know I don't deserve it, but I guess I've learned that the hot guys aren't the ones to trust."

It felt like old times, except Cindy was so humble and so contrite.

I looked around the cafeteria, and didn't like what I saw. "He's coming over," I warned her.

"Really?" Cindy looked up hopefully as Sean approached our table.

"I want my book back," he said curtly, and sat down on our table, practically on top of my lunch.

"What book?" Cindy asked. "I never took one of your books."

"Oh, yes, you did. You took it out of my backpack when you were climbing all over me in the football field."

Cindy's eyes filled with tears. Other people at tables nearby turned their heads and looked at us.

"Give it back," he shouted. "It's that stupid one, *Pride*—"

"*Pride and Prejudice*!" I shouted back at him. "And it's not stupid, and you're sitting on my lunch. So get lost and stop bothering us. You're making a fool of yourself."

"Hey!" he stood up and looked at me angrily. "I wasn't talking to you, so shut your mouth, and tell her to give me my book."

"I don't have your book," Cindy wept. "I never had it."

I stood up and yelled, "Now, you leave her alone, you jerk, and get away from here! You've got some nerve, picking on a girl like Cindy, and making her cry."

My fists were clenched and I moved toward him. He was easily a head taller than me but he backed off.

"And you don't even have enough sense to appreciate a masterpiece like *Pride and Prejudice*. And what a bird brain like you is doing in an Honors English class is beyond me."

He retreated, and then said in a lower voice, "I'm not in an Honors English class, and the book is *Pride of the Yankees*, so stop yelling."

"I don't have your book," Cindy repeated.

Now I began to feel foolish. It was one thing to defend *Pride and Prejudice*, but *Pride of the Yankees* was something else.

Sean lingered. "Okay, Cindy, I apologize. Maybe I left the book home or maybe I lost it. I love baseball, but I hate reading about it. Anyway, why don't you introduce me to your friends."

"Uh, this is Jenny Chu, and this is Alice Burns."

Sean sat down next to me, and I moved away.

"Glad to meet you, girls," he said. "Those cookies look good," he added, and took a few out of my sandwich bag.

"I didn't offer you any," I said.

Sean smiled. "You're really a little firecracker, aren't you. Well, I like a girl with spirit, so—"

I stood up and said to Jenny and Cindy, "I'm going off to the library."

"So am I," said Jenny.

"Me too," said Cindy.

And we left him sitting there.

"Wow!" Cindy said as we walked upstairs to the library.

"I never thought you had a temper like that, Alice. I think he's interested in you. I bet he'll chase after you."

"He'd better not," I told her. "And I hope you can see the kind of creep he is."

Cindy decided to go to her locker while Jenny and I headed off to the library.

"I guess she'll be eating with us after this," Jenny said sadly.

"And maybe Kevin, too, when he gets back to school, and maybe his friend Jeff," I told her, "which is what I've been trying to talk to you about. You know Jeff Lyons in my P.E. class?"

"Who?"

"Jeff Lyons."

"Oh, he's the genius, right?"

"Well, he's very smart. You remember Kevin and I went to the New Year's Eve party at his girlfriend's house?"

"Jeff Lyons has a girlfriend?"

"Well, he's broken up with her, and I thought . . . I mean,

I mentioned you to him, and he'd be interested in getting together with you."

"Me?"

"He's really a good kid, and never mind how he looks today, but I thought if you were interested, maybe the four of us—Kevin, Jeff, you, and I—could get together one day and hang out for a while."

Jenny wrinkled her face thoughtfully. "He's not very cute, is he?" she asked.

"Oh, but he's a good dancer."

"Jeff Lyons is a good dancer?"

"Jenny," I said, "it's a mistake to judge a person on first impressions. Let's just get together when Kevin gets back to school. Jeff can be a lot of fun, and I'm sure he'd like you."

"Well, okay," she said, smiling, "but don't tell Cindy."

CHAPTER 21

I called Kevin as soon as I arrived home from school.

"Hello!" he rasped.

"Oh, Kevin," I said, "you sound terrible."

"I can talk a little, though," he whispered hoarsely. "You'd better do most of the talking. How's school? Did you get the homework?"

"I got it for English, and Jeff gave it to me for math and science. And, oh, Kevin . . ." I started laughing and couldn't stop. "Oh, Kevin . . . it's Jeff . . . He . . ."

"Well, what?" Kevin rasped irritably.

"Kevin . . . he . . . Jeff . . . he dyed his hair. It's sort of a fuchsia red, and he's wearing low-rise jeans. He said Maggie made him do it. But he told her he wouldn't wear a nose ring. Oh, he looks so funny! And he's broken up with her, and I thought maybe he and my friend Jenny could get together. She's really his type. But he looks hysterical with his fuchsia hair."

"I wouldn't do that for anybody!"

"How about me, Kevin?" I giggled. "Why don't we both dye our hair green?"

"Give me the homework, Alice," he whispered, sounding cranky.

"You'd look good with green hair," I laughed.

"Oh, shut up, Alice! You just don't know when to stop," he croaked.

"Can't you take a joke?" I yelled into the phone.

"No!" came a furious whisper, and Kevin hung up.

I sat there looking at the phone. Call him right back, a

voice inside me urged, *and apologize*. But I didn't want to call him back. I wanted him to call me back. After all, what did I say that was so terrible? Just a little joke about dyeing his hair. He should have known I didn't mean it.

After five minutes, I realized he was not going to call me back, but I sat there anyway. Was this it? Just a vacation romance? Call him back, the voice said again. But the other voice said it was obvious that he didn't have a sense of humor, and didn't care about me at all. Maybe he was just waiting for a chance to dump me. Maybe he never really liked me. Maybe . . .

After ten minutes, I got up, went into the bathroom, locked the door, and cried until Rosie jiggled the knob and said she needed to go.

Ms. Herran was standing by her desk the next morning when I showed up early for class. "Here, Alice," she said, handing back my paper. She sounded so serious that I worried maybe I'd gotten it wrong again. Quickly, I glanced down at the first page. It said "A+," with a bunch of comments, which I didn't read then. She was talking to me softly, ". . . best paper I've read in years . . . so insightful . . . so appreciative of the humor and the style. It's a good thing you read it over again. And so well written, you must have spent hours and hours on it."

"Yes, I did," I admitted. "Pretty much a whole day. I think *Pride and Prejudice* is the best book I've ever read."

"You know," Ms. Herran said, "I'm going to have to read it over again. You pointed out in your paper something I had never thought about before—why Mary is so important to the story just the way she is."

"Yes," I agreed. "That's what I came to understand."

"A lesser author might have tried to come up with some kind of romance for her, might have changed her as all the other sisters change. But leaving her as she is makes the book much more realistic. Boring people don't change. A good writer doesn't have to tie up all the loose ends."

"Well, I tried," I told her, "but it didn't work."

"What?"

"I mean that's what I thought should happen in the book. But I was wrong."

Ms. Herran didn't seem to hear me. "Mary balances the book," she said. "Thank you, Alice, you've given me something new to think about."

"I think I'm going to be a writer," I told her. "But I guess it's not going to be easy."

"Well, that's good news," she said as the bell rang, and she turned into everybody's English teacher again. "Paul, please shut the door! Diana, pick up that tissue you just dropped, and Ryan, will you please distribute these papers?"

I sat down, clutching my A+ paper to my chest. The rest of the day passed for me in a haze of misery.

It didn't help that Sean Murray stopped me in the hall.

"Hey, Alice, how's life?"

"Pretty rotten," I said, moving along.

He fell in step beside me. "Well, maybe I can help make you feel better." He was leering at me as if he expected me to just fall down at his feet and tell him how happy I was he'd even condescended to talk to me.

So I stopped walking and looked right up at him. "Somebody like you could never make somebody like me feel better," I told him. "So just go away and bother somebody else."

"Listen, Alice," he said. "You have the wrong impression of me. I don't know what Cindy told you, but honestly, she just kept chasing after me. So maybe I was a little rough with her, but—"

"Rough with lots of girls, from what I hear." I began walking again. "I have to go to math."

"Who told you that?" he asked, walking along with me.

"Never mind. Somebody dependable."

"You know, I can't help . . . well . . . looking the way I do."

"You remind me of a character in a book I love. His name is Wickham. He's so good-looking that lots of women fall for him. But he's a real scumbag like . . . well . . . I've got to go."

"You know, Alice," Sean said, "this guy—whatever his name is—he can't help himself. He's got all these girls running after him. It distracts him."

"That's no excuse for making girls feel bad, and boasting about them to your friends."

"Okay, okay, but they were all silly girls. Maybe if I ever met a girl like . . . well, a girl who was different, maybe I could be different too. I could try."

He looked so helpless standing there, like one of my little brothers. Someone like Sean would never change, and I almost felt sorry for him. So I patted him kindly on the shoulder and said in my big-sister voice, "Okay, Sean, you keep trying. I wish you luck."

"And maybe, Alice, you and I could get together after school, and you could give me some advice."

"Sorry, Sean," I said as the bell rang, "I'm busy and I'm late."

As I galloped along to my math class, I thought, Sean Murray, the alpha male in the school, was actually asking—

almost pleading—for a date. At another time, I might have been thrilled, but I hoped I would have said no. All I wanted now was for Kevin to stop being angry with me.

CHAPTER 22

I hurried home. The boys were playing computer games upstairs. I could hear them arguing over whose turn it was to pick and who picked one last time and the time before—the usual. I could hear Mom singing in the kitchen, but I didn't have the time to talk to her.

Thank goodness, nobody was on the phone. I grabbed it, and then hesitated. Should I call him? Should I sound as desperate as I felt? Suppose he hung up again. Suppose he said, "Look, Alice, we're through." Could I face that kind of humiliation?

Quickly I dialed. The phone rang once, and Kevin answered it. His voice sounded almost normal. "Hello!"

"Hello, Kevin, it's—"

"Alice, listen. Alice—"

"I'm sorry, Kevin. I wanted you to know how bad I felt. Please don't think I really meant it—I mean, about dyeing your hair green. You know I—"

"Alice," Kevin said. "I've been sitting here in front of the phone waiting for you to get back from school. I was going to call you in four and a half minutes. I didn't sleep last night. I kept thinking how stupid I was."

"No, I was the one who was stupid. You were sick, and I should have understood you weren't in the mood for joking around."

"I should have called you back right away. I don't know what got into me. But, Alice, you know, Alice, if I didn't have you . . . it's hard to say this, but my life would be totally empty."

"Yes!" I cried. "That's the way I feel. Oh, Kevin, I'm so glad you're not angry with me."

Making up was wonderful. We kept apologizing back and forth and assuring each other that we'd never, never argue again. I couldn't wait to see him.

"I hope you're coming back to school tomorrow," I said.

"I sure am, and I can hardly wait. I . . . I miss you, Alice . . . I . . ."

"I miss you too, Kevin. Oh, I got an A+ on my *Pride and Prejudice* paper."

"Do you want me to read it?" Kevin asked without much enthusiasm.

"No, Kevin. You read the book for me. I can't expect you to do any more."

"I'm glad, Alice. I'd certainly read it if you wanted me to, but I think I'm ready for some science fiction stories. Eleanor promised to go to the library yesterday, but she forgot."

"I could go for you. Just tell me which authors you like."

"It's okay, Alice. I'll be out of here tomorrow, and I can pick my own books."

"Why don't we both go tomorrow after school? I want to read another book of Jane Austen's. I want to read all of them. But this time, I'm not going to change a single word. I can't wait until tomorrow. I'll see you then."

"And the day after," Kevin said. "And the day after . . ."

Mom was singing, "Goin' to the chapel and we're gonna get married." She was stirring something in a pot and looking at a recipe on the worktable next to the stove.

"What are you cooking, Mom?"

"Oh, hi, Alice." Mom had been using more makeup lately, and I noticed she was wearing a new apron with different-colored grapes. "It's a recipe your grandmother, Dad's mother, used to make. It's—wait a minute—it's called Chicken Tetrazzini."

"Chicken what?"

"Tetrazzini." Mom turned to smile at me. "And guess what, Alice? Dr. Berger is giving me a raise. He says the atmosphere in the office is so cheerful lately, even the patients who need root canal are more relaxed."

"Jeremy and Joey won't eat it," I said, peering into the pot.

"Well, I think I need to expand my cooking horizons," Mom said, stirring again. "I can always pop a few hot dogs in the microwave for the boys, but it's time I thought about what your father likes, and the rest of you too, of course. And by the way, I will need some butter, but it's okay, Alice. I'm sure you have lots of homework. I'll ask Olivia to go to the store this time. Actually, the boys are old enough now to help. Maybe I'll ask one of them."

"I can go, Mom," I said. "What do you need?"

Mom ended up needing a pound of butter, a half gallon of milk, a jar of marmalade, and a roll of paper towels. I rounded them up, feeling happier than I'd ever felt before when I had to go to the store. Even though the package was heavy and the weather cold and drizzly, it struck me that I was starting the new year as a different person, a new me.

And then the bus passed. She was on it, wearing, of course, her hooded raincoat. But this time, she was smiling at me from whatever I could see of her face, and waving. I waved back.

No one knows what Jane Austen really looked like. We have one crabby portrait done by her sister, Cassandra, and a water-color, also done by Cassandra, showing Jane Austen dressed in a bonnet and pretty dress, but, sadly, from the back. From time to time, fans come up with portraits of pretty women that they insist are newly discovered pictures of her. But invariably, they all turn out to be somebody else.

So the mystery about her appearance continues. More than fifty years after her death, her nephew, J. B. Austen-Leigh, describes her in his *Memoir*: "In person she was very attractive; her figure was rather tall and slender, her step light and firm, and her whole appearance expressive of health and animation. In complexion she was a clear brunette with a rich colour; she had full round cheeks, with mouth and nose small and well formed, bright hazel eyes, and brown hair forming natural curls close round her face." But he was a boy when she was alive, and his description may be somewhat cloudy.

I like not knowing what she looked like. It forces me to find her in her books—six of them with six different heroines. I hope she looked like Elizabeth Bennet in *Pride and Prejudice*—pretty, slim, with brown hair and bright, sparkling, "fine" (as Darcy describes them) eyes. But, more important, I know what kind of person she was from those six books, frag-ments, and about one hundred and fifty letters.

She never married, although her delightful letters describe her crush on a young man her age (about twenty-one) named Tom Lefroy. Later in life, he admitted that he had "loved Jane Austen," but added, "with a boy's love." He was certainly married at that time and perhaps feared that his wife would not approve.

We also know that another man proposed marriage to her, and at first, she accepted him. But the next day, she changed her mind, fled back home, and remained there with her beloved sister, Cassandra, and her mother for the rest of her life.

Jane Austen lived in England from 1775 to 1817. She wrote six novels, and one of them, *Pride and Prejudice*, has become not just a classic, but also a story that has been read and enjoyed for nearly two hundred years. Most readers can find themselves or people they know in one or another of the sisters.

Over the years, a number of movies have been made about *Pride and Prejudice*, including an Indian one called *Bride and Prejudice*. Other authors have written sequels, unwilling to let the characters slip away. There are organizations all over the world where members meet to discuss Jane Austen, her books, and anything that remotely relates to her. One of the organizations, here in the Bay Area of San Francisco, was started by the author of this book.

I am certainly not alone in my admiration of Jane Austen. To some, her fans are considered fanatics, dangerously close to lunacy. But there are many of us, and the number of her admirers increases as the years go by.

I hope that those of you who read *First Impressions* will go on to read *Pride and Prejudice*. It is one of my favorite books by my favorite author.

Jane Austen comforts me when times are hard, and she reminds me how funny, precious, and delightful this world is, as well as the people (or most of them) in it.

MARILYN SACHS

116

I feel lucky to have her in my life. And I hope I can share the magic of reading her books with you.

—M. S.

The edition of Pride and Prejudice *referred to in* First Impressions *is the 1998 Oxford World's Classics paperback edition, edited by James Kinsley.*